PRAISE FOR *UNDER THE SUN*

'*Under the Sun* is a moving and original drama that illuminates subtly the human face of war' Patrick Bishop

'A profoundly moving and gripping story, *Under the Sun* is a small masterpiece; the best novel that I have read about war since *Captain Corelli's Mandolin*. It can well stand the comparison' Nigel Jones, *Sunday Telegraph*

'This well-researched and thought-provoking novel skillfully explores the psychology of conflict and the contradictions and absurdities in the wartime concept of "the enemy". It is an impressive first novel that grippingly depicts the suffering and pain of conflict, and the humanity that lies within us all' *Japan Book Review*

'The gripping and beautifully paced debut of an intriguing new talent' William Dalrymple

'Recommended, and an author to watch' *The Bookseller*

'Book of the month' Foyles

Under the Sun

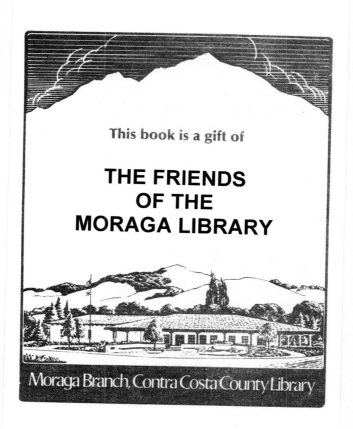

This book is a gift of

THE FRIENDS
OF THE
MORAGA LIBRARY

JUSTIN KERR-SMILEY was born in 1965 and brought up in Scotland. He was educated at Ampleforth and read history at the University of Newcastle upon Tyne. As a foreign correspondent he has reported from Northern Ireland, the Balkans and South America. *Under the Sun* is his first novel.

JUSTIN KERR-SMILEY

Under the Sun

ARCADIA BOOKS

Arcadia Books Ltd
139 Highlever Road
London W10 6PH

www.arcadiabooks.co.uk

First published in the United Kingdom by Reportage Press

This edition published by Arcadia Books 2013

Copyright Justin Kerr-Smiley © 2013

A catalogue record for this book is available from the British Library.

ISBN 978-1-908129-49-9

Typeset in Minion by MacGuru Ltd
Printed and bound by CPI Group (UK) Ltd, Croydon CR0 4YY

Arcadia Books supports English PEN *www.englishpen.org* and
The Book Trade Charity *http://booktradecharity.wordpress.com*

Arcadia Books distributors are as follows:

in the UK and elsewhere in Europe:
Macmillan Distribution Ltd
Brunel Road
Houndmills
Basingstoke
Hants RG21 6XS

in the USA and Canada:
Dufour Editions
PO Box 7
Chester Springs
PA, 19425

in Australia/New Zealand:
NewSouth Books
University of New South Wales
Sydney NSW 2052

in South Africa:
Jacana Media (Pty) Ltd
PO Box 291784
Melville 2109
Johannesburg

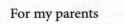

For my parents

'A wraith of cloud lies on the fringe of night,
And as a bird sweeps over the lost earth
I hear the cry that is its solitude.
Now silent as the cross at windless noon
The coral sands that spread beneath me lie.
O would that it had been the sun that caught
My friend, exiled from light, whose fate recalls
Young Icarus, the illustrious aeronaut
Who tumbled headlong down the marble sky...

Always as now, I shall remember him,
Feeling the rapturous stillness of the stars,
When across sleeping fields the shadows swim.
Always as now.'

Ian Davie 'Aviator Loquitur'

'Concerning martial valour, merit lies more in dying for one's master
than in striking down the enemy.'

Tsunetomo Yamamoto 'Hagakure'

'The thing that has been, it is that which shall be; and that which is
done is that which shall be done; and there is nothing new under the
sun.'

Ecclesiastes 1:9

ONE

The sun rose beyond the island. A breath of wind stirred the leaves of the coconut palms that lined the airstrip, their fronds sashaying together in a dance. On the breeze came an odour of raw fish, hibiscus and engine oil: the smell of the tropics. The runway faced eastwards, pointing towards the rising sun like a blade, its surface covered with sheets of pierced steel planking because of the monsoon. Lined up along the airstrip were the sixteen Mark VIII Spitfires of 607 Squadron, the planes arrayed in clusters of four, the backs of their sleek bodies arched against the increasing light, so they looked like a school of porpoises breasting the surf. The airfield was deserted except for the sentries guarding the main gate and the duty officer up in the wooden control tower. Sitting in his wicker chair the officer yawned and stretched and looked across at the empty runway. Out of the gloom a figure wearing flying kit emerged from one of the huts and began walking towards the aircraft. It was the pilot of the dawn patrol.

Before the Allied victory in Europe, the squadron had always gone out in pairs and most often in fours, but with the fall of Berlin and the Japanese defeat at Guadalcanal and Iwo Jima the war, which seemed to have gone on for as long as anyone could remember, was now almost at an end. The once feared Imperial Japanese Airforce was no longer a threat and the main purpose of 607 Squadron's patrols was to support Allied advances in the region and harass any Japanese shipping unwise enough to find itself caught in the open sea. It was only a matter of time until the Showa Emperor and his cohorts around the Chrysanthemum throne capitulated. Or so everyone, including Flight Lieutenant Edward Strickland, liked to think.

The pilot paused and took a Player's from its packet. He put the cigarette to his lips, flicked open a lighter and lit it, enjoying the tobacco smoke that filled his lungs before replacing the lighter and packet in the top pocket of his shirt. He stood and stared at the ascending sun, its rays penetrating the gold clouds of the horizon, reaching out across the sky like a many bladed fan. It reminded him of benediction at school when the priest held up the monstrance containing the Blessed Sacrament, while they all bowed their heads. It was a moment of epiphany, the sunlight falling in slabs through the tall windows, the clouds of incense dusting the air with myrrh, the pale candles flickering on the altar, the choristers' voices filling the church with song. And now at dawn on the other side of the world here was another, albeit different, benediction. Standing alone on the runway, Strickland bowed his head, but this time before the sun god. He stood up and stubbed out his cigarette and walked towards his plane.

The ground crew were making their final preparations to the Spitfire, when they caught sight of the tall figure striding towards them. The pair took a step back and saluted the young officer, who returned the greeting.

'Morning Jenkins, morning Watson.'

'Morning Mr Strickland,' they replied.

'Nice day for it,' said Jenkins.

'Let's hope so,' answered the pilot.

Strickland ducked down to check the plane's undercarriage and walked around the back to look at the rudder and the ailerons. Satisfied, he went to the front and inspected the nose cone and the propeller, before rounding the wing and climbing up into the cockpit. He got in and placed his parachute beneath him and sat down. Jenkins, the fitter, helped strap him in while Watson, the rigger, stepped out in front of the aircraft, waiting to guide the pilot onto the runway. Having done up the harness Jenkins patted Strickland's shoulder and wished him luck. The officer murmured his thanks as he attached the oxygen mask to his face and pulled the goggles down over his eyes. He made sure the ground flight switch was set to ground; fuel on; brakes on (air pressure sufficient); magnetos on; radiator fully open; RPM lever forward and throttle set half an inch open and ready to start. Strickland waved, signalling that everything was correct.

'Contact!' he called.

The rigger looked about and saw the Spitfire was clear.

'Contact!' came the response.

The pilot simultaneously pressed the start button and boost coil and the Merlin engine gave a cough, spluttered into life and began to roar. He checked the dials on the instrument panel: engine revs, oil pressure and temperature. Everything was fine. He opened the throttle gently, watching the RPMs on the rev counter and placing his feet on the rudder pedals, he checked the tail rudder in the cockpit mirror. He then glanced at the ailerons on either side, working them up and down with the joystick. Strickland stared at the runway ahead of him, the sun rising above the ocean, the dawn sky framed by his canopy window. The pilot waved away the chocks and opening the throttle a fraction, he released the brakes and pulling the stick back into his stomach, he nosed the plane out onto the airstrip.

Through the whirring circle of his propeller, he could see Watson motioning him on until he was out in the middle of the runway. The rigger stepped aside with a final wave and in his ear phones Strickland heard the officer in the control tower telling him he was clear for take-off. The pilot thanked him and the voice wished him 'bon voyage' as he opened the throttle fully and eased the stick forward, lowering the nose and feeling the aircraft picking up speed. In front of him the engine growled and smoke belched from the twin banks of exhaust stacks on the cowling, the plane's wheels racing across the steel planking. After three hundred yards the Spitfire left the ground, floating gracefully upwards; an unwieldy beast on land now becoming a winged chariot in the air. Flying with his left hand, Strickland moved the metal lever with his right, raising the undercarriage, and a red light with the word 'up' illuminated on the left-hand side of the instrument panel. He pulled the RPM lever aft reducing the revs for the climb, checked the controls and felt the plane swing briefly from side to side as it rose like a lark into the dawn sky.

After throttling back to climb power, the pilot looked down at his compass and took a bearing of seventeen degrees east, swinging out across the lightening sea, before turning inland and flying back over the flat corrugated roofs of the camp. Beyond the houses the jungle-clad mountains rose up green and massive, the valleys and canyons filled with a low, pale cloud that would soon dissipate. As the sun rose above the mountains patches of forest steamed, the Spitfire climbing all the time as it traversed the dark heart of the island, a thin trail of condensation flowing in its wake.

There were stories that the interior of the country contained tribes who had never set eyes on a white man. If they were true, Strickland wondered what these people must think of the great metal birds that roared and swooped above them. Would these people run and hide, or would they drop to their knees in fear, raise their arms in supplication and beg for mercy? It was a strange thought and he hoped they would not be too afraid.

The pilot continued on above the mountains, keeping the canopy open so that he could feel the morning breeze upon his face. He did this out of habit and not simply because he sought relief from the enervating tropical heat.

Some years before during the long, hot summer of 1940 Strickland had a lucky escape above the hop fields of Kent. After a dogfight in which he had shot down a Dornier, he was preparing to return home when he was jumped by a Messerschmitt 109. He had been so excited shooting down the bomber, his first solo kill, that he briefly relaxed, failing to look in his cockpit mirror as he followed the stricken plane to the ground, ignoring everything he had been taught in the euphoria of the moment.

The pilot only realised he had become the prey when he saw a line of tracer streaking past his starboard wing. Having spent all his ammunition on the Dornier he had none left, but Strickland was sure he could outmanoeuvre the slightly quicker Me-109, so long as he kept low and hugged the contours of the land.

Try as it might the Spitfire could not shake off its pursuer, who stuck resolutely to its tail. In his mirror the pilot could see the yellow-nosed Messerschmitt in close pursuit, small flames erupting in its nose and wings each time the enemy fired his cannon. His adversary was no novice and he decided to climb for a thick bank of cloud so as to lose him. The move surprised the German and Strickland had almost reached the mass of cumulus, when a burst of gunfire hit his aircraft. The plane heaved and shuddered like a stricken horse and flames poured from the engine, the cockpit filling with choking black smoke. After trying the controls Strickland knew there was nothing he could do except bale out and he quickly unstrapped himself and attempted to pull the canopy open. But a piece of shrapnel had struck it during the attack and the casing would not budge. With flames now pouring into the cockpit he desperately tried to prise it open, tearing his gloves off in order to get a better grip on the release catches. In mounting panic he struggled in vain to free the canopy, yet it refused to move. He reached down and grabbed the crowbar in the cockpit door, but his hands could not grip the burning metal. With flames licking all around, the pilot pushed the aircraft into a steep dive in a bid to blow the fire out. Instead the steepness of the descent increased the smoke, causing him to black out and the next thing Strickland knew, he was falling free from the aircraft.

Somehow the gravitational forces had pulled the canopy open and he dropped out, shelled like a pea from a pod, as the plane flipped over on its back. As he tumbled through the sky the pilot regained conciousness and pulled his parachute cord, the silk canopy opening above him in a great white bloom. He raised his eyes to check his lines were not twisted and then looked about.

The Messerschmitt had disappeared into the blue and Strickland floated earthwards like some fallen angel. It was only as he descended that he became aware of the pain in his hands and saw the skin on them was raw and blistered like seared meat. The pilot landed safely in an apple orchard and after convincing a pitchfork-wielding farmer with some forthright Anglo-Saxon that he was not a member of the Luftwaffe, but a flight lieutenant in the RAF, he passed out again.

He woke up a day later to find himself in hospital, his body swathed in bandages. His face and hands had been scrubbed and sprayed with tannic acid which had formed into a thick black scab, while his eyes had been bathed and swabbed with gentian violet. He lay there in bed wrapped up like an Egyptian mummy, with two holes for his eyes and another for his mouth. Fortunately, Strickland's head and face had been protected by his goggles and helmet and the burns, although painful, were superficial. Unfortunately his hands were a mess and would require several operations.

The doctors kept him full of morphine to dull the pain, so the days passed in a blur of pale floating shapes and gentle murmurings, as he lay mute and bound in his bed. In those first few days Strickland remembered only the whiteness of the hospital ward and the hushed voices of the nurses, as they flitted to and fro like anxious moths. He was mostly delirious and often suffered from nightmares. Either he was struggling to get out of his burning aircraft, or he watched helplessly as another pilot was attacked by an enemy fighter. He would shout and scream at his fellow aviator to no avail and could only look on horrified as the plane burst into flames. After one such dream Strickland woke to find three orderlies holding him down as a nurse administered an injection. Eventually, the amount of morphine in his system was reduced and the fog that had enveloped him lifted and his mind no longer wandered quite as much as it did. But there was nothing they could do about the nightmares, which continued for some time.

Strickland's parents visited as soon as he was well enough to see them and he remembered his mother being brave as she stood at the end of his bed, trying not to cry. He made some lame joke about being like the Invisible Man and that when they finally removed his bandages, there would be nobody there. The surgeon had been kind enough to laugh, but he could see his parents did not find his predicament in the least bit amusing. There was a look of anguish on his mother's face when he announced that he hoped he would be back flying again soon. The surgeon merely smiled and said he should take each day as it came.

As his strength returned the pilot was able to sit up and talk and he always remembered the kindness and diligence of the sisters who tended the ward. There was one man who had crashed during take-off on a training flight, his plane cartwheeling across the end of the runway, blazing like a Catherine Wheel before exploding in a sheet of flame. As the rescue team pulled him from the burning wreckage it was said the skin on his arms came off like a pair of gloves. It was a miracle the man had survived and like every other burned pilot, he was taken to the same special unit for life-saving surgery. The place was much like any other hospital, where people came in grievously wounded and either left through the front door, or else in a long wooden box out the back. The only difference with the burns unit at East Grinstead was that there were no mirrors. And when the nurses removed the bandages from the novice's face you knew why. Even the other patients had to turn away, the sight was so terrible. But the medical staff were unabashed. Only once did a nurse faint and she had been new. With or without a face, the young flier was treated with the same care and dedication as everyone else.

Another regular visitor for Strickland was his commanding officer Archie Lambton, a bluff pipe-smoking Lancastrian and an accomplished cricketer who had played for his county. He also captained the squadron's XI and the flight lieutenant opened the batting with him. The two of them regularly had a partnership of a century or more, the wing commander invariably chalking up at least fifty. One afternoon Lambton arrived and pulling up a chair, he sat down and told his subordinate that he had some good news. He had recommended him for a Distinguished Flying Cross.

'Whatever for?' the pilot asked, genuinely surprised.

Lambton was taken aback at this response and began to bluster that he was a valuable member of the squadron, had at least one confirmed kill and had shared in another two, as well as having another probable to his name. Strickland nevertheless saw through the man's blandishments and realised the decoration was intended as compensation for his injuries. He knew he did not deserve the medal, but his CO plainly did not expect him to take to the wing again. It seemed he would be deskbound for the rest of the war. Even so, Lambton was as good as his word and three weeks later Strickland's DFC was gazetted, his parents proudly showing him the announcement in *The Times*.

In the days and weeks that followed, the pilot was able to move about and spent much of his convalescence walking in the large grounds of the hospital, enjoying the fine autumn weather. The gardens were well tended and he liked to stroll along the gravel paths clad in his pyjamas and dressing gown, stopping occasionally to sniff the sooty perfume of a rose. The weather that October was unusually mild and the trees were clothed in red and gold. Leaves idled earthwards and birdsong echoed through the woods. To pass the time patients played chess or bridge and wrote letters home.

Christmas came and went and New Year was notable only in that the bandages on Strickland's hands were finally removed, after the last of his many operations. It meant he could now visit the local pub along with the other walking patients, since he was no longer at risk of infection. On his first visit to the Dorset Arms in the high street, he had been ordering a round of drinks when he noticed a familiar figure staring at him from behind the counter. He thought it was a ghost until he recognised with a shock that he was looking at his own reflection in the long mirror behind the bar. It was the first time he had seen his face in months and as he glanced at his friends carousing around him, he realised how fortunate he was. They too must have seen their own disfigured faces as they took their turn at the counter and yet somehow they had all come to terms with their injuries. Not one of them had ever complained about their disfigurement and Strickland was humbled by their fortitude.

After almost six months at East Grinstead the pilot was given his discharge papers, returning to his squadron in early March. Two brother officers, George Hay and Harry Armstrong, collected him on the day of his release in Armstrong's Morris Oxford. The hospital staff stood on the steps and waved him goodbye, as did the other patients who were allowed out from their wards. The trio set off and leaving the sleepy Sussex village they made their way to London, passing through the bombed-out areas of Lewisham and Battersea before arriving in the West End. They had a fine lunch at Simpson's in the Strand where they drank champagne and dined on oysters and roast beef, before setting off for the airfield in the late afternoon.

Strickland sat on the back seat with his cap on his knee, his uniform newly cleaned and pressed, the purple and white ribbon of his DFC sewn above the left breast pocket. As they raced through the narrow Kent lanes he felt glad to be back on active service after his weeks of confinement and subsequent rehabilitation, although he doubted he would be allowed to fly again because of his injuries. Along the sunlit verges crocus and primrose bloomed and blackbirds flitted in and out of the damp hedgerows.

As the pilot day-dreamed, the two men in front chattered away. The blond and ruddy-faced Hay was now officially an ace with five confirmed kills to his credit, while the slighter and darker Armstong had three. Both of them had a DFC, while Hay had recently been awarded a DSO. Lambton and the young trio were now the only remaining members of the squadron who had flown in France, covering the troops' retreat at Dunkirk. The other eight had all been killed.

The mountains slid away beneath the Spitfire as it flew out across the open sea, the pilot scanning the ocean with his eyes as he looked for any signs of enemy shipping. He turned his aircraft due north and watched as the sun rose up into the morning sky, its light a hammer beating down on the flat anvil of the sea, the plane and its occupant a speck in the heavens. Alone at the controls the pilot gloried in his solitude. Instead of the muddy fields of Waterloo or Flanders, his battles were played out amid this empty plot of sky. Not for him the life of an infantryman fighting in the desert sands of North Africa, or slogging through the Burman jungle with rifle and pack. Instead, his arena was one of boundless blue. As a knight and his charger, so the pilot and his aircraft. Man and machine in harmony together.

The pilot continued flying north and headed towards the Carolines, a myriad of islands and coral atolls, which gave some protection to the enemy ships and submarines that plied the area. There were markedly fewer ships these days, but plenty of submarines which were always elusive. At night among the islands they would surface unseen and take on fresh water and supplies, before slipping out to sea again. The Carolines were at the limit of the Spitfire's range, but they were also the most fruitful hunting grounds for the squadron. And so each day the pilot from the dawn patrol would make a sortie, choosing his favourite haunts which he knew his quarry preferred, like a fisherman who knows where the best salmon pools lie. And just like a fisherman sometimes his patience and skill would be rewarded and equally sometimes it would not.

After two hours flying at ceiling altitude Strickland pushed the stick away from him and the Spitfire descended towards the ocean. At 2,000 feet the pilot levelled out and up ahead he could make out the irregular contours of the Carolines along the horizon. In a few minutes he was flying over them, circling the archipelago that lay scattered across the sea below, like a string of pearls on a dark cloth. Each island was a forest of palms and in the heart of some there rose an occasional mountain, usually an extinct volcano. The Carolines had been the enemy's Pacific base from the beginning of the war until 17th February 1943, the Japanese Year of the Sheep, when American carrier planes swooped down on Truk which was home to the Combined Fleet. In the attack they destroyed seventy planes on the ground and sank two auxiliary cruisers, an aircraft ferry, two submarine tenders and twenty-three merchant ships. It was the biggest Japanese loss since the battle of Midway the previous year.

Strickland began to search among the scattered islands and atolls, looking for the tell-tale wake of a ship or a submarine as it ploughed across the blue. He also kept an eye on his fuel gauge, making sure that he did not spend too long on his quest and not leave himself enough to get back to base. Checking his watch, the pilot saw that he could spend a maximum of five minutes in the area, before he would have to head for home. He searched both port and starboard, dipping the plane's wings from time to time to get a better view.

The waves crashed against the atolls in a ring of white surf, but the pilot could see no wake from any ship. Here and there he spotted the tiny sailing rigs of fishermen, their wooden vessels bobbing about in the ocean like corks. Flying low over one of the boats, Strickland saw the fishermen raise their straw hats and wave and he waggled his wing tips in reply as he flew on. He glanced at his watch again and at his fuel gauge, which hovered at the halfway mark. A minute more and he would have to return to base. He put his foot down on the left rudder pedal and swung the plane to port, as he rounded one of the larger islands for a final sweep.

The pilot had almost given up his search and was thinking thoughts of home, when he noticed a thin white trail cutting through the waves on his starboard side. It was probably nothing more than an outlying reef breaking the surface and he pushed the stick away from him and dived towards the sea to take a closer look. As Strickland neared the spot he could see the line was too straight to be a reef or a rocky outcrop and yet there was no sign of any ship. It was strange. Then he saw why and his heart flipped inside his chest like an eel in a trap. Just beyond the whirring yellow rim of his propeller blades he could see the distinct outline of a Type C submarine, the letters I-47 stencilled on the conning tower. It must have been at the island he had just flown over and was making for the open sea again. Tensing with excitement Strickland knew he had his prey and he shuffled his feet on the pedals and wheeled his plane round to attack.

The aircraft swept across the sea towards its quarry, the pilot's thumb resting on the brass firing button. Pointing the nose of the Spitfire a little ahead of the submarine's bow so as to give it sufficient lead, Strickland peered through the reflector-sight and fired a burst, the four 20 mm cannons on the wings stuttering in a roar. Small white splashes flayed the water around the submarine, as the plane screamed overhead and turned to make another pass. As the Spitfire banked sharply a group of sailors leapt out from a hatch and ran towards the gun on the upper deck. The pilot levelled his aircraft and came in for another run, the cannon blasting away and tearing up the water in front of him. But this time the crew were ready and he noticed black puffs of smoke erupting around his canopy as the submarine's 50 calibre gun returned fire. Strickland kept his line and concentrated his aim at the base of the conning tower, the aircraft bucking slightly with each burst. Again he flew low over the enemy vessel, passing just a few feet above, before banking the Spitfire and turning in a wide circle as he lined up for the kill.

The pilot raced across the waves once more, the submarine a sharp silhouette in his gunsight. He pressed the firing button and saw the bullets streaking ahead, knifing the water and ripping mercilessly into the steel hull. The bow gun continued to fire, its muzzle flashing methodically with each round as the

Spitfire approached. With a shriek the aircraft hurtled overhead, the gunners frantically wheeling as they blasted away, black puffballs of smoke dotting the sky around the plane as the flak exploded. Suddenly the aircraft lurched and veered sharply to one side and a cry went up from the crew. A thick trail of smoke poured from beneath the plane and the gunners began to shout and leap about, as they watched the Sptifire yaw from side to side before climbing away.

Inside the cockpit Strickland remained calm as he turned the plane round and headed for home. He knew he had been hit and although the controls were soggy, the aircraft was still manageable and he thought that he could make it back. But he was being unduly optimistic. While the Spitfire still responded to his movements, a quick look at the fuel gauge showed him that it was on zero. The submarine's gun had ruptured the fuel tanks on the wings and he was doing no more than flying on empty. The pilot searched in vain for an island where he could beach the plane, but none lay ahead. As he looked about for a suitable landing site the engine began to run roughly, the fuel mixture in the carburettor evaporating. With a final cough the engine died, the propeller spinning to a stop. Strickland was too low to bale out and drifted in a silent glide. He levelled the plane and flew parallel to the waves' crests as he prepared to ditch in the sea. As the Spitfire dived towards the ocean, he undid his parachute and tightened his harness straps, bracing himself for the impact. A moment later he hit the surface, the sea erupting in a geyser around him. Water gushed into the open cockpit, his body jerking against the harness as the plane slewed to a halt. The Spitfire was still and the water subsided, the plane rocking gently in the waves.

Strickland quickly undid his straps and removing his sodden parachute, he climbed out onto the aircraft wing, taking the Very pistol and a box of shells with him. He loaded and cocked the pistol, pointed it at the sky and pulled the trigger. There was a sharp retort followed by a puff of smoke as the flare rose in an arc and the pilot watched it drop still flaming into the sea. He knew it was unlikely he would be rescued, but it was possible there were friendly vessels in the vicinity and the flare would at least alert them that someone was in trouble. Strickland put the pistol in his pocket and reaching down into the cockpit, he pulled out the life raft and his heart sank. There was a long tear across the middle, presumably made by a piece of shrapnel. He threw it aside and opened a panel in the fuselage and took out the box containing the survival kit, which was undamaged. He then inflated his Mae West and sat down on the wing with the box on his knees, his legs dangling in the tepid water.

Strickland undid the top pocket of his shirt, took out his packet of cigarettes, put one in his mouth and lit it. The cigarette was damp, but it smoked well enough and he sat there listening to the waves slapping against the aircraft's hull, as he pondered what to do. It was doubtful anyone had seen the distress signal and without a life raft, he would be too small to spot from the air. Strickland could see the island was some distance away, probably three or four miles; but he was a good swimmer and thought he might be able reach it, so long as the current did not drag him in the opposite direction. There was not much of a choice. Either he sat there and went down with the plane, or else he tried to swim to the island. If he stayed where he was, his bones would soon join the pale mass of coral which lay just a few fathoms below.

Strickland took a final drag on his cigarette and tossed the stub away. He removed his helmet and goggles and took off his shoes and the now wingless Ariel slid off the Spitfire into the water. He began to paddle towards the island, one arm helping him swim, the other clasping the survival box. He turned around only once, when he heard a gurgle and a rush of water and saw his aircraft tip slowly forward and sink beneath the waves. When it had disappeared Strickland turned back again and continued swimming. After a while he abandoned his grip on the box which was hampering him. Later, he pulled out the bulky Very pistol from his pocket and disposed of that as well. With his arms now free he swam in a breaststroke, his limbs working away in unison, the island rising up tantalisingly from the surf ahead.

Every now and then Strickland would rest and try to establish how far he had swum. Each time he did so the island appeared to be just as far away as before and he began to wonder if he was making any progress. After an hour's hard swimming and with the island apparently no closer, Strickland stopped and started to tread water. He realised he was not going to make it, the current was too strong. With the sun burning mercilessly in the heavens and the waves constantly splashing into his eyes making them sting, he knew he could not swim any further. Exhausted, he lay listlessly in the surf like a jellyfish at the mercy of the tides. He looked down at his Mae West, which was the only thing keeping him afloat. He could stay like this for hours, or even days and then what? To go mad and die of thirst like some shipwrecked mariner or else be eaten by sharks. Surely drowning was preferable? Strickland reached into a pocket and pulling out a penknife, he opened it and slashed his life jacket in half, the air escaping with a hiss.

TWO

Standing on the jetty and peering through a pair of binoculars, Captain Tadashi Hayama had been watching the circling Spitfire for some time, praying that it would not discover the submarine. It seemed as if the gods had answered his prayers, when he saw the enemy aircraft finally veer away and head for home. Then it turned again and to Hayama's consternation, he watched it bank before making a steep dive. Moments later he saw the Spitfire's cannon flashing and heard the roar of gunfire above the crashing surf. To his satisfaction he also heard the louder boom of I-47's bow gun, as the submarine tried to fight off its attacker. He looked on, a fascinated spectator, as the plane turned and dived again, the submarine's gun firing in a constant barrage. His satisfaction turned to delight when he saw smoke pouring from the aircraft's fuselage. He stood and watched as the plane pitched and crashed into the sea, the soldiers around him laughing and cheering.

The pilot, if he was not dead already, would have been killed by the impact and Hayama knew that he and his men were safe. The submarine had come and gone and could now continue its glorious work against the enemy. Hayama gazed out towards the horizon again, but there was nothing except the sunlit sea, endlessly shifting and turning with the tide.

The captain addressed the man standing next to him.

'The gods are with us, Noguchi.'

'They are with us, sir, because we honour them,' replied the sergeant.

'I shall make a special offering at the shrine this evening,' said Hayama and his subordinate gave a brief bow.

The captain turned to leave, and just as he was about to depart one of his men shouted and pointed in the direction of where the plane had ditched. Hayama stopped and looked and to his dismay, he saw a flare rising up into the blue sky. The pilot was not dead after all and even worse, he expected to be rescued. The area was crawling with enemy ships, someone was bound to see the distress signal and come looking. They might even get as far as the island.

Hayama knew he had to search for the pilot. Whatever happened the man must not be rescued and allowed to give away the island's position. The captain and his men had lain hidden there since the beginning of the war. While all around him the other larger islands had fallen to the marauding Americans, the Japanese officer's own haven had gone undetected. The island had not been attacked, because nobody knew they were there. For the past four years C Troop, 68th Signal Regiment had acted as a vital listening post for the Combined Fleet. Each day they tracked enemy aircraft and noted the position of passing ships and every evening Hayama relayed this information back to his superiors in Osaka, who would then pass it on to the submarines which still patrolled the Carolines.

Angrily the officer addressed Noguchi.

'*Oi gunso!* Get the boat ready! We must find that pilot. He must not be allowed to get away!'

'*Heitai-san,*' replied the sergeant, saluting sharply before turning and ordering his men to board the patrol boat moored alongside.

The soldiers swarmed onto the boat and began to cast off ropes, while others went below to prepare the engines and get the vessel underway. Hayama waited and was the last to step aboard. As the gangplank was hauled in behind him, the engines gunned into life and the boat surged out from under the palms into the still, clear waters of the harbour. The captain went to the bow and stood poised like a figurehead, his legs braced against the stanchion as he leaned into the breeze, the binoculars raised to his eyes. He faced in the direction of the plane, but all he could see was the white surf crashing over the reef.

The boat left the calm waters of the harbour and negotiated the narrow channel that led through the coral barrier, before heading out into the open sea. Hayama remained at the bow, the breeze plucking at his khaki britches, the binoculars to his eyes as he cast his gaze over the water in front of him, the boat rising and falling with the ocean swell. All the time he kept saying to himself: 'I must find the pilot!'

After a while Hayama put out an arm, signalling the crew to slow the boat's engines, as they began to patrol the foaming surf. The sun glanced off the bright water, making them squint as the men looked about for any sign of the plane or its occupant. Despite the captain having correctly observed the Spitfire's position when it crashed, it had already sunk by the time they arrived. Hayama cursed quietly and lowered his binoculars before looking back at the island and again at the sea surrounding him, certain he was in the right place. He ordered the boat's engines to be cut and the vessel shuddered to a halt. The only sound was the surf and the wind moaning in the rigging as they floated silently on the waves, and he raised the binoculars to his eyes once more and began methodically to sweep the area.

There was nothing out there. All the captain could see was the constant rise and fall of the ocean and he began to think that perhaps the pilot had gone down with the plane after all. He could have been wounded and unable to get out. The flare might have been the last desperate effort of a dying man. Yet Hayama could not be sure. He must make certain, or as certain as he could be, that the pilot was not out there somewhere. If the pilot were ever picked up, it would be the end of their operation on the island. There would be no one left to spy on enemy aircraft and shipping. The captain turned and ordered the crew to start the engines again and search the area once more, telling his troops to spread out along the boat's gunwales. He offered a week's pay to the first man who spotted the pilot. For the next three hours they trawled back and forth, the engines throbbing rhythmi-cally above the surf as they pitched and rose upon the swell. Occasionally, in his eagerness to please his officer, a man would cry out that he saw something and Hayama would run round with his binoculars and scrutinse whatever it was the man was pointing at. It was always a trick of the light. There was nothing out there. The pilot was surely dead, or even if he were alive, he would not be for long. Either way the sharks or the sea would get him. The captain looked at his watch and saw that it was now past midday. It was dangerous to stay out any longer, there could be an enemy air patrol at any moment and if they were spotted, the whole point of searching for the pilot would be lost.

Hayama turned and walked towards the boat's cabin. He was about to order the vessel back to the island, when a shout came from the other side.

'*Taiisan, taiisan*! I can see somehting ahead. It's the pilot, I'm sure. Yes, it's him! I am certain of it!' As the captain raced towards the stern, other men began to shout and gesticulate.

'Yes! Look! There he is in the water!'

'Where? Where?' demanded Hayama as excited as his men, but unable to see what it was they were pointing at.

'Right there, *taiisan*,' said the private who had first called out.

The officer put his binoculars to his eyes, as he followed the man's finger pointing at the waves. He looked and saw nothing at first, just the brilliant sea endlessly turning and falling. Then a body wearing a yellow life jacket could be seen floating a hundred yards away, the blond head lolling to one side. It was the pilot. Hayama ordered the boat to turn around and running back to the bow, he directed it towards their quarry. The boat drew up alongside the airman, who did not move or show any signs of life. A corporal grabbed a boat hook and lowering it over the side, he caught the man's life jacket as he lay motionless in the water. Together the soldiers heaved the limp body over the rails and deposited it on the deck, so that it lay there like some sodden piece of jetsam.

The captain squatted on his heels to take a closer look. He saw the RAF's winged insignia on the shirt and noticed from the bars on the epaulettes that the man was a flight lieutenant. So he was a British officer. He looked more dead than alive and Hayama put a hand on the pilot's neck, to see if there was any movement in the jugular vein. He felt a faint trembling beneath his fingertips, like the beat of a butterfly's wing. There was barely a pulse. He called for some water and a soldier produced his canteen.

The captain opened it and poured some into his hand, splashing it over the pilot's face. He then tipped the bottle into the man's mouth, the water streaming down his chin. There was a moan and Hayama brought up his hand and slapped the man hard across the face, but he did not respond. He took out a silver case from his tunic and shook out two white pills onto the palm of his hand. He opened the man's mouth and putting the salt tablets on his tongue, he washed them down with some more water from the canteen. Having done this the captain ordered his soldiers to place the pilot on a stretcher and to put him in the shade. He took out a handkerchief from his pocket and soaked it in what remained of the water and laid it on his captive's forehead to keep him cool. Then he got up and told the crew to head for home.

The patrol boat sped back towards the island, the sun burning in the heavens as the vessel rode the foaming surf. Hayama stood on the gunwale watching over his captive, who lay silently in the shadows. He tried to calculate how long the man had been in the water and thought that it must have been at least four hours. The Japanese officer was surprised he had lasted so long, seeing that his life jacket was torn and concluded that he must have considerable strength. He wondered if the pilot had been trying to swim towards the island. If he had his efforts would have been futile. The current was strong and flowed in the opposite direction.

It was late afternoon by the time the vessel made its way back through the reef and headed into the safety of the harbour. The sky was beginning to deepen and the trees' shadows lengthened across the water. When they reached the jetty, Hayama supervised the unloading of the stretcher and ordered his men to take the pilot to his own quarters. The captain led the way as the soldiers trudged down the wooden boards of the pier onto the white beach, the sand making them stagger drunkenly as they walked. With the pilot slung between them they stumbled up the slope and into the trees, taking the path that led towards the camp. The men reached Hayama's quarters and carried the stretcher up the steps and through the door, putting it down in the middle of the room. The captain dismissed them and when they had gone, he knelt down next to the motionless body of his prisoner. He put his ear close to the man's mouth and listened to his breathing. It was was more of a sigh than a gasp.

Hayama sat back and observed the pilot. He had never seen an enemy this close. In fact he had never actually seen an enemy in person before, only aircraft and ships and they had always been at a distance. Now here he was face to face with his adversary and he was unsure what to do. Should he take out his revolver and shoot him? He was the enemy after all. Somehow it did not seem right to kill a man who was unconscious and apparently dying. And if he did not shoot him, what was he going to do with him? Interrogate him certainly, if he survived. But then what? Execute him? Keep him prisoner? The captain really had no idea.

A voice interrupted his thoughts and looking up he saw his orderly standing by the kitchen door.

'What is it, Ito?'

The young man bowed courteously and answered.

'*Taiisan,* I was wondering whether you would like some refreshment? Tea perhaps?'

'Yes, tea would be nice.'

'And what about?' and the orderly indicated the prone body of the pilot with a nod of his head.

'The prisoner is fine for the moment, thank you,' replied Hayama with a weary smile.

The orderly left and soon returned carrying a tray with a teapot and cup. The man set it down on Hayama's desk and bowing once more he departed. The Japanese officer got to his feet and going over to his desk, he poured himself some tea. He raised the cup to his lips and drank its steaming contents. The jasmine was sweet and refreshing and its fragrance soon began to mollify him. He tipped the cup back and finished it, and then poured himself another. Hayama looked across at the pilot lying on the stretcher. There was nothing else he could do. Either the man would come round or he would not. He suspected the latter. If he died everything that he knew would die with him. And yet the pilot might well have given their position away. He would have to wait and see. Whatever happened it was out of his hands.

'So be it,' muttered the captain.

He pushed the tea tray to one side and sat down at his desk. Hayama then removed a sheet of paper from a drawer and began to type up a report of what had happened, beginning with I-47's arrival the previous evening. He made an inventory of all the stores the submarine had taken on board and the amount of fuel and fresh water the vessel had required. Hayama also reported on the morale of the crew which he described as excellent. He paused as he remembered their exhausted and unshaven faces, their oil-smeared clothes and their sour breath and crossed out the word '*sugureta*' and replaced it with '*subarashii*', or fine. The crew of I-47 should have been relieved weeks ago, but because of American advances in the region and the subsequent destruction of their own shipping, every vessel and crewman of the Combined Fleet was needed. The submarines were only allowed to return to the mainland if they were irrevocably damaged.

The captain described the Spitfire's attack on I-47 and how the crew's quick response had enabled them to shoot down the aircraft. He knew his superiors would enjoy reading that, especially as this would be corroborated by the commander's own version of events. It was not often that a submarine from the Combined Fleet could paint an enemy aircraft's silhouette on its conning tower. Hayama also mentioned that he had searched the area to see if there was any sign of the plane and wrote, truthfully, that there was none. He stopped typing and turned to the figure lying on the stretcher and wondered if he should say that he had found the pilot, but thought better of it. If they gave him an order, he would be obliged to carry it out. They could not give an order about something which they did not know. And besides the man would probably die anyway.

Hayama leant back in his chair and emitted a low sigh. There was something else, something that he did not understand and it vexed him. Why did he not feel animosity towards his enemy? Throughout his life, and certainly since he had been in the army, he had learned to be wary of Occidentals and their devious ways. They were inferior to the Japanese in every respect, worse than dogs some of them. Uncivilised, ill-educated and arrogant. This he knew to be true. And yet he did not despise this man as he really should. Hayama rubbed his forehead. It made no sense at all. He sincerely hoped the man would die.

He returned to his report and finished with a paean to the Emperor and the Motherland. After reading it through once more, he tore the sheet of paper from the typewriter and got to his feet.

'*Oi, joto-hei!*' he called.

There was a sound of someone running, followed by a clattering up the wooden stairs and a soldier appeared at the doorway and saluted.

'I am going to the signals hut to make my report. Watch over this prisoner until I come back. If he comes round give him some water. But only a little. Report anything to me immediately.'

'*Heitai-san,*' said the private as he stepped into the cabin. He went over to where the pilot lay and stood to attention next to him, his rifle by his side.

Hayama folded his report, put it in a pocket and left his

quarters, making his way across the compound to the path that led down to the harbour. Tall grey palms towered above the khaki figure as he walked, their canopy shading the trail. Above him the branches were filled with the cries and chatter of monkeys, as they ran like shadows through the trees. The path opened onto a broad strip of beach and the captain strode across the sand to the water's edge. He stood there looking out to sea and watched as the evening sun descended towards the horizon in a blazing stream. He remembered the evenings at his home in Nagasaki and how he would watch the sun set over the harbour there, the fishing boats floating on a sea of fire. It was high summer now and the parks and squares would be full of children playing. The jacarandas and the magnolias at the Kofukuji Temple would have shed their flowers, but their leaves would still be lush and green. He wondered if he would ever see the cherry blossom along the Nakajima river again. Or indeed his family. He had had no contact with his parents, or with his brother or sister, since the Pacific war began. His sister was a nurse and had been stationed in the Philippines. He had had no news of her since the island had been taken by the Americans. His younger brother was a naval aviator and had been based on the carrier *Hiryu*. But the ship had gone down at Midway, so he could well be dead. The captain stood there facing the horizon, the waves washing upon the shore. Such thoughts made him melancholy and he tried to banish them from his mind.

Hayama looked down and saw a coconut bobbing at the water's edge and he began to sing softly to himself.

From a far off island whose name I do not know
A coconut comes floating.
How many months have you been tossing on the waves
Far from the shores of your native island?
I think about tides far away
And wonder when I will return to my native land.

The captain stopped singing and across the water came the happy sound of laughter as his men took an evening dip, diving off the end of the pier. Hayama watched his soldiers and smiled. How he wished he could be carefree like them. He would have loved to join in, but such intimacy was forbidden. An officer should never become too friendly with his men. They respected him because he kept his distance. And so he let the soldiers continue with their horseplay, not wanting to spoil their moment of abandon. The day would come when they would no longer be able to lark about anymore and that day was forever drawing closer. They had endured countless experiences together and he would miss them when the time came. He knew it would not be long now. Hayama realised that Japan could not win this war. But as a samurai he knew there was victory in death.

As the descending sun sank towards the horizon, the captain left his men to their evening bathe and went off to file his report. The signals hut lay hidden above a cove on the other side of the island. It faced north as there was a good reception from the mainland. Hayama walked along the shell-strewn beach, his boots crunching across the sand. Scattered about were the skeletons of starfish and the bones of squid and cuttlefish, as well as the pearly shells of various molluscs. With the sea at their door, there was never any shortage of food for Hayama and his men. In the early days on the island they would often make a fire on the beach and sing songs by the light of the moon. They could not do that now.

Hayama continued along the seashore and made his way through the forest above the bluff, which overlooked the harbour. He went up a low hill and walking over the crest, he descended to the other side. Below him he could see the signals hut with its tall aerial rising up through the trees. It was a simple place no bigger than a chicken coop, its roof covered with palm fronds. The captain trotted down the narrow path to the cabin, whistling as he went.

Inside the signals hut were a corporal and another private.

It was quiet and both men had their feet up, listening to music from Radio Tokyo. Hayama was a little earlier than usual and when he entered they leapt to their feet, bowing and apologising as they did so.

'It's all right, Corporal Higa,' said the officer. 'There's still ten minutes to go … please sit down. You too, Private Kamiko.'

Bowing again both men sat down and the captain pulled up a chair. Higa turned off the radio and put on a set of headphones, flicking switches and plugging in leads in preparation for the broadcast. On the wall was a clock, the long hand a fraction away from the hour. They waited and chatted in the remaining minutes. At precisely eight o'clock Hayama began to read from his piece of paper, Higa tapping out the code with his morse key, the room filling with the sound of the brass contact as it click-clacked away. In a couple of minutes the report was finished and thanking his radio operators, the captain got up and stepped outside.

His work now done for the day, Hayama went off to the shrine to make his offering. It lay just below the signals hut in a natural cave and consisted of no more than a wooden Buddha sitting in a lotus position on a throne, his right hand raised palm outwards in a blessing, the other resting in his lap. The soldiers had erected a wooden temple around the god to keep off the rain and had painted it in blue and gold lacquer. The paint was now peeling in places and the structure was so rudimentary that it had been shored up with timber to prevent it from collapsing. But in its rustic simplicity there was also an honesty and purity, which would have pleased any deity.

When he got to the shrine the captain took out his petrol lighter, flicked it open and lit some incense sticks, before putting the flame to several small candles at the Buddha's feet. Then, removing his forage cap, he placed his hands at his sides and bowed his head and gave thanks for the day. He prayed that he would do his duty as a loyal son of the Motherland, as a servant of the God Emperor and as a samurai. And he prayed that if

Buddha willed it, he would be allowed to join his ancestors in heaven. Hayama stood there for a while, his head bowed before his Lord.

By the time the captain had finished praying, it was almost dark. A scattering of stars lit the heavens and a new moon rose above the palm trees. He left the shrine and walked back through the forest towards the harbour. Hayama descended the bluff and saw the luminous crescent of the beach glowing between the trees. When he reached the lagoon he strolled along the shore, the oily water lapping the pale rim of sand. In the warm darkness came a scent of frangipani. The captain sighed and breathed in deeply, relishing the smell. As he stood there sniffing the night air, he noticed dark shapes wheeling and tilting across the night sky. Hayama watched the bats as they flitted about searching for insects, swooping and diving above his head. He tried to follow their jinking flight, losing them as they turned away into the forest, only to see them reappear as they raced across the water, the air filled with tiny shrieks. There came a deeper cry, a low chirring, as a nightjar called for its mate. The captain listened as the bird made its plaintive song: a series of sharp notes, repeated again and again. Eventually the nightjar flew off into the darkness and silence resumed, the surf ceaselessly scraping the shore.

Hayama left the beach and took the path through the trees that led back to the camp. As he approached his cabin he could see the windows' amber glow and knew his orderly had lit the lamps. He ascended the steps and went inside and was welcomed by the guard snapping to attention. The captain had almost forgotten about his prisoner and looked at the pilot lying moribund on the stretcher.

'Has he come around?'

'No sir!'

'Did he say anything?'

'Not a word, sir.'

'Has he moved?'

'No sir, nothing.'

'Very well, private. You are relieved. Go and get some supper.'

The soldier saluted his officer, made a quick bow and marched out of the hut. The captain watched him go, before turning his attention to the prisoner. The pilot lay at his feet, his breathing measured, his body still.

'What are we going to do with you?' he muttered.

Hayama looked away and called out to his orderly. In a moment Ito appeared from the kitchen, bowing and wiping his hands on his apron.

'Yes, captain?'

'Is supper ready?'

'Yes, captain.'

'Then bring it to me. It's been a long day and I'm tired.'

'Right away, sir,' and bowing again the orderly went back to the kitchen.

Hayama took off his sword and placed it reverently on the rack above his bed. Then he sat down and began to unlace his boots. He put them to one side and stripping off his uniform, he picked up a white silk kimono and put it on and for the first time that day, he began to relax. He took up the violin which lay next to his bed and after wiping some resin across the bow, he placed it between his knees and began to play. He drew the bow back and forth across the strings, the violin's shrill music haunting the air. And as the captain played he also sang, the room filling with the sound of his voice.

Light green they shine
Dark green they shine,
Stretching into the distance as far as the eye can see,
They glitter like jewels.
Oh, how they glitter – those low hanging boughs
Of the willows on Suzaku Oji...

Hayama continued singing and was so immersed in his music, that he did not notice the orderly place his supper on the table beside him and depart again. The captain was lost in his reverie and as he closed his eyes and sang he imagined he was back in his native land; with its great forests and bamboo groves, its mountains and its rivers. There was nowhere quite as beautiful as the land of Yamato. Hayama played on, the violin's melody like the mosquitoes which rose up in clouds during the summer months. And as he played his eyes brimmed with tears, which poured down his cheeks. But they were not tears of sadness, they were tears of joy.

Eventually the captain stopped playing and wiping his face with his sleeve, he put his violin to one side and looked at the fare laid out before him. There was a bowl of rice, some raw fish, a bowl of water chestnuts, another containing shredded seaweed, a dish of soy sauce and a small brown jug of *sake*. Hayama sat down, reached out for the jug, poured the rice wine into a cup and drank its contents in a single gulp. The wine warmed his stomach and he poured himself another cup, then picked up his chopsticks and began to eat. The captain had had nothing since breakfast and was hungry. He took a piece of raw fish, dipped it in the soy sauce and ate it, washing it down with the *sake*.

Hayama soon finished his supper and he rinsed his fingers in a bowl of water and shook them dry. The captain then got up from the table and began turning out the lamps. He left one on by his bed and went over to the door and stood outside on the porch, looking up at the new moon. The same moon would be hanging over the harbour at Nagasaki, the water glinting in its light like the shards of a broken bottle. He knew his parents would be looking at the moon and thinking of him, just as he did of them. His father old and bowed and yet still wiry and strong, forever the samurai. His mother kind and smiling and so pretty. She did not look a day older than in her wedding photograph. What a fortunate man he was to have such parents!

The camp was quiet and most of the lamps were out, with just a couple still burning in the darkness. Soon they too would be extinguished and the men would be asleep. The captain went back inside and shut the door. He walked over to his bookshelf and removed a volume of poetry, then sat down next to the prisoner, who had not moved or uttered a sound since he had been brought in. Hayama bent over and put an ear to the man's mouth. The pilot was breathing faintly and he thought that since he had lasted this long, perhaps he might survive after all. The captain sat back and pulling his kimono tightly around him, he prepared himself for a long vigil. He opened his book and began to read from one of his favourite poets, the seventeenth-century Shinto priest Matsuo Basho.

Breaking the silence
Of an ancient pond,
A frog jumped into the water
A deep resonance.

Hayama continued reading, the pilot lying on the stretcher beside him. Outside a nightjar called in the darkness, its solitary song echoing in the forest.

THREE

All night the captain sat reading and watching over his captive, waiting to see if he would move or make a sound. But there was nothing. Finally, in the still, quiet moments before dawn, before the sky had become light and the birds had woken, Hayama fell asleep. His head nodded forward and the book spilled from his hands into his lap. He breathed evenly and deeply, echoing the man that lay beside him. While the captain slept, the body on the stretcher started to move and twitch. In his dreamings the pilot began to wake, his conciousness effortlessly rising to the surface like phosphoresence. And as his body moved and twitched, he started to moan. The sound increased until it was interrupted by a shout and both men woke with a jump.

Wide awake Strickland found himself staring straight into the eyes of a Japanese officer. Hayama sat there looking at him, both of them momentarily stunned. Not surprisingly, since the pilot had remained unconscious for all that time, it was the captain who came to his senses first.

'You are a prisoner,' he announced.

Strickland looked at him and wondered how he understood the words and as his captor repeated them, he realised he was speaking English.

'You were shot down. We rescued you.'

'Shot down …?'

'You attacked the submarine. They shot you down.'

'The submarine …' repeated Strickland vaguely.

'We came and rescued you. You were in the water.'

The pilot blinked in the lamplight. His eyes hurt and his head ached. Although he remembered seeing and attacking the submarine, his mind was blank after that. The Japanese officer said he had been shot down and that he had been in the water. But he could see he was not aboard any ship. So where was he? It did not make any sense.

'Where …'

'Where?'

The pilot struggled. He was still groggy from his ordeal and because of his parched throat, he found it painful to speak, his voice a faint croak.

'How … did I get here?'

'We came and rescued you.'

'Why?'

'It does not matter.'

The two men continued to look at each other. The captive and the captor. There was a silence, before Hayama spoke again.

'You must be thirsty.'

Strickland swallowed and nodded and the captain got up and went to the pitcher, which stood on a table by the window. He poured some water into a glass and returned and squatting down, he handed it to his prisoner. The pilot propped himself up on an elbow and leant forward, and taking the glass he raised it to his blistered lips, greedily drinking the water. In a couple of gulps it was gone and Strickland gave back the glass. As he did so Hayama noticed the scarring on the pilot's hands, but said nothing.

'That is all you can have for now,' he said, putting the glass to one side. 'Here take these,' and the captain produced his little silver case. He tipped out two more salt tablets onto his palm and gave them to the pilot. Strickland popped them into his mouth and felt them dissolving on his tongue. But his mouth was still dry and he was unable swallow.

'Water,' he pleaded.

The captain shook his head.

'Later, but now you must rest.'

The pilot was exhausted and it hurt to think. He still did not understand. Why had the Japanese come and rescued him? What were they doing here? And where exactly was he? He could not answer any of these questions and he was sure that had he asked, his captor would not have told him and so he lay back on the stretcher and closed his eyes. In a short while he had fallen asleep, his breathing calm. The Japanese officer watched over him. He would live, that was certain. The man was too weak to interrogate now. He would do so in the morning after he had rested further and he went over to his own bed and started to undress. When he had finished Hayama raised the mosquito net and naked, got into bed, pulling the sheet over him.

And so the two men slept out the remainder of the night, although it was Hayama who woke first. As the early morning sun filled the cabin, the Japanese officer slipped out of bed and went to the basin to wash. He poured some water into the bowl, picked up the soap and began to scrub his body. His back was broad and muscled and his legs were strong. It was the lean, capable body of an athlete. Hayama lathered himself all over and taking a cloth, he rinsed it in the water and started to wash the soap from his limbs. He stood there feeling refreshed and renewed and proceeded to wipe away the remaining water with his hands.

After tying a towel around his waist, he picked up a comb and ran it through his fine black hair. He wished he could grow it long and knot it behind his head as his ancestors had done, but military regulations stipulated short back and sides. As he combed his hair the captain looked into the little mirror which hung by the window above the basin. His chin was darkened by stubble. He replaced his comb, picked up the bar of soap and his shaving brush and lathered his face. He took up his razor, dipped it into the bowl of water and began to shave, drawing the blade down in long, even strokes. He then rinsed away the soap and dried his face with a cloth. Hayama looked in the mirror again, drew a hand across his cheeks and found them smooth. He took off his towel and picking up his clothes, he started to dress. The captain buttoned his tunic and sat down on the bed and put on his boots. He did up the laces and stood up and stamped each foot, shaking out the creases from his britches.

The noise woke Strickland. He opened his eyes and was confronted by the sight of a Japanese officer standing before him in full military uniform. Momentarily he was as confused as he had been the night before. Then the pilot remembered where he was.

'How are you feeling?'

'Fine ...'

'Fine is good,' and Hayama turned and called out to his orderly. '*Joto-hei, koko ni kinasai!*'

In a moment Ito appeared at the kitchen doorway, a small boyish figure with glossy black hair dressed in a neatly pressed servant's uniform and a white apron. He stood there and tried not to look at the tall Englishman who had got to his feet and stood towering over the two Japanese.

'*Asagohan o watashita ni onegaishimasu,*' said the captain.

'*Heitai-san, ima sugu ni!*'

The orderly promptly left and in a few moments returned with a tray of breakfast and Hayama indicated that the Englishman should come and join him at the table. The pilot did as he was told and sat down on the tatami opposite his captor. Ito placed two small bowls in front of them and two pairs of chopsticks. There followed a plate of chopped mangoes, a bowl of rice, some steamed egg and bean curd, a pot of tea and a jug of fresh goat's milk. The captain then dismissed his orderly and poured them both a cup of tea.

'Eat,' he said, waving his hand at the food.

Strickland obeyed and helped himself to some rice. He spooned some of the egg and bean curd onto it and picking up the chopsticks began to eat, sipping from his cup of tea between each mouthful. Hayama did the same and they ate for a while in silence, both men watching the other, but each trying not to catch the other man's eye. The game continued for a while, as the two of them warily observed each other, like a pair of wild animals in a cage. Eventually the captain put down his chopsticks, wiped his mouth with a napkin and spoke.

'What is your name?'

The pilot stopped eating and lowered his chopsticks and looked at his adversary. But he did not reply. Hayama frowned and asked the question again.

'I asked you what is your name?'

'My name is Edward Strickland.'

The captain nodded and repeated the words.

'Ed-ward Strick-land.'

'Yes …'

'And you are a flight lieutenant in the RAF …'

'That's right.'

'You were flying a Spitfire. Which squadron do you belong to?'

The pilot looked at the captain and shook his head.

'I'm afraid I cannot tell you. I can only tell you my name, rank and date of birth …'

There was a sudden crash as the captain's fist struck the table, sending the bowls and teapot flying and knocking over the jug, the milk spreading in a pool across the oiled teak.

'*Baka inu!*' he swore. 'You are my prisoner and you will answer my questions!' The captain's brow twisted with rage, his face flushing with anger.

'I am a prisoner of war and I only have to tell you three things. Two of which you already know and as for the other …'

'*Damara butayaro!*' swore Hayama, pounding the table again with his fist and upsetting the plate of mangoes into the pool of goat's milk.

The pilot looked at the Japanese officer and saw that he was extremely angry. He still felt weak from his ordeal and was in no shape to take a beating. Even so, he knew he must not divulge anything that could be of use to the enemy. He also realised that pride was at stake. His captor had first beguiled him by taking care of him and giving him breakfast, in the hope that he would betray the name and location of his squadron and any other useful information he possessed. Beating or no beating Strickland was determined to remain firm. The battle of wills between the men continued, immutable force meeting immoveable object. Finally, the pilot spoke.

'By the way, you haven't told me your name.'

Hayama sat there and blinked. What was this? Was this man perfectly crazy? Did he not realise that not only was he a superior officer, he was also a samurai? That he should in truth get up, pick up his sword and split him in two like an apple. The prisoner's impertinence was astounding. As the captain sat there contemplating what he should do, he recalled the teachings of the samurai master Tsunetomo Yamamoto: that a fight was something that went to the finish and that a man who forgot the Way of the Samurai and did not use his sword, would be forsaken by the gods and the Buddhas. That both men should be crucified as an example to subsequent retainers. Hayama was about to get up and fetch his sword, when he remembered another piece of advice from the master: that a samurai, when faced with a crisis, should put spittle on his earlobe and exhale deeply through his nose. If he did this he would overcome anything.

Now it was the Englishman's turn to be amazed as instead of being struck down, as he fully expected, his captor licked his forefinger and thumb and began gently to rub his ear. Even more extraordinary was the smile which spread across the captain's face as he did so.

'My name is Tadashi Hayama,' he said.

The pilot nodded, his captor's rage seemed to have passed with the sudden violence of a summer storm. He surveyed the table betweeen them, with its mess of broken crockery and food. Hayama's anger had swept like a hurricane through a forest, knocking leaves and branches to the ground and turning rivers into cataracts, but leaving the rest of nature intact. Now the forest was still again, the only sound being the distant gushing of the river and the steady drip of rainwater.

'Why did you rescue me?'

'It does not matter,' said the Japanese officer, still smiling.

The pilot was right, the captain was perfectly calm, his rage had passed and he sat there with all the serenity of a Buddha. The two officers observed each other for some time, saying nothing. Eventually Hayama spoke.

'You do not wish to talk?'

'No.'

'So be it.'

Hayama sighed and called out and Strickland heard the sound of people running. Turning he saw a pair of figures in khaki, clattering up the steps and enter the hut. They stood there in the doorway and bowed simultaneously at their captain.

'*Taiisan, nannano?*'

Their officer looked at them and indicated his prisoner with a tilt of his head, before uttering a single command.

'*Boukou!*'

The Englishman did not understand the word, but he soon understood its meaning as the guards approached and began to rain blows down upon him. Both men taking turns to strike his head, face and body. The guards were systematic in their punishment and took care with their aim, going unerringly for the body's vulnerable parts especially the liver, kidneys and testicles. Strickland did his best to ward off the blows, but there were too many and he was reduced to rolling himself up in a ball in an attempt to protect himself. The soldiers continued to rain punches down upon him and only ceased when the captain gave the command.

'That's enough!' he ordered. 'Get him out of here.'

The guards stopped their beating and taking a foot each, they dragged the pilot out of the hut and down the wooden steps. They hauled him across the compound and took him to the storeroom and opening the door they threw him inside, bolting it behind them. One of the soldiers then stood by the entrance and kept watch, his arms folded across his chest.

Hayama surveyed the damage of the breakfast table and tutting to himself, he told his orderly to clear it up. He went over to the wall and removed the long sword from its bracket and put it on. The prisoner was lucky he had not being wearing the weapon during their confrontation, as he would certainly have used it. The captain checked that his sword was hanging properly and putting on his cap, he went outside. The first interrogation session had been a disappointment, but he would not be thwarted again.

Strickland lay there in the darkness, his face and body battered, the metallic taste of blood in his mouth. He spat and a mixture of bloody saliva and pieces of tooth dribbled onto the earthen floor. Tenderly he touched his gums to check the damage and on the upper right-hand side of his mouth, he felt the gap where a molar had been. He prodded around to check his other teeth and was glad that he had not lost any more. He felt his nose, which was badly smashed. Even touching it made him wince with pain. His left eye was swollen and shut, but his other eye was undamaged and with it Strickland surveyed his new prison. The walls were made of bamboo, lashed together with vine and the roof was solid timber. In the gaps between the bamboo, golden shafts of light fell. In a corner lay a pile of mealy bags and next to them were a stack of barrels.

The pilot crawled towards the bags to see what was in them and opening one, he pulled out a handful of rice. He began to open others, and found they only contained rice or beans. He went over to the barrels and found them all sealed. There was some Japanese writing on the side, but since he did not know the language he could not decipher it. The wood smelled faintly of alcohol and he presumed they were filled with wine. Strickland retreated to his corner and sat down on the ground, pulling his knees up to his chest. Although his body hurt and his head ached, the beating had not broken his spirit. On the contrary it made him even more determined to resist. He refused to give in to his captor. He realised he would die here and he did not care.

He should have died many times before. He should have died in France. He should have died above the hopfields of Kent. He should have been killed like so many of his other comrades had been. All of them brave men and all of them gone.

The pilot knew he had run out of lives long ago and that it was only a matter of time before he too was lured like Orpheus into the underworld, unable to resist the siren call of Eurydice and the gods' strange music. He was quite prepared to die, or as prepared as any man could be and being a combatant in war, he was more prepared than most. If there was one thing that troubled Strickland as he sat there alone in the gloomy storeroom, it was that Hayama had not left him to drown. Had his captor done so he would have quietly slipped beneath the waves and that would have been it. The pilot was sure the captain had his reasons, but he would never know. Whatever they were it did not actually change anything, since he might as well be dead. He only had one desire and it was this: that he would not break during any further interrogation. With this thought in his mind Strickland lay down to sleep and soon he was transported far away from the tropics and the island that had become his prison.

The pilot's dreams were filled with the faces and voices of his dead comrades, as they emerged unbidden into his subconscious like a host of bright angels. It was during the fall of France and he and his brother officers were sitting in deckchairs, enjoying the early summer sun. A breeze stirred the flowering limes that lined the airfield and the air was drowsy with the hum of bees. On the wind came a scent of dog rose, hawthorn and elderflower, along with a tang of manure from the byre. Standing upon the farmyard midden, a scarlet-combed cockerel raised its head and let out a full-throated cry.

The retreat at Dunkirk was still a month away and they were playing cricket against a neighbouring squadron. Strickland's team had already bowled out the opposition and now it was their turn to take the wicket. Padded up and swinging his cricket bat so as to loosen up his shoulder, the young flight lieutenant walked out to the crease along with his opening partner Archie Lambton. The duo made an incongrous pair as Lambton, then a squadron leader, was squat and dark and clasped his bat firmly under his arm while his blond, willowy companion whirled his around his head like a farmhand with a flail.

When they got to the pitch they took up their positions at opposite ends, with the younger of the pair taking the strike. Strickland aligned his bat against the stumps and called for 'middle and leg' and when the umpire indicated that his bat was in the right place, he used it to score the hard ground in front of the wicket. Lambton stood nonchalantly at the other end, leaning on his own bat as if it were a shooting stick and apparently without a care in the world. His partner looked on as the bowler prepared his run up, gently tapping his bat against the side of his boot. As Strickland did so he kept his eyes fixed on the bowler who waited for the umpire to drop his arm before starting to run, racing ever faster towards the wicket as he raised his arm and let the cricket ball fly from his hand. The ball hurtled down the pitch, striking the ground a yard in front of off-stump and went whizzing past Strickland's bat straight into the hands of the wicket keeper. The bowler was deceptively quick and his pace drew ironic comments from the slips, but the batsman ignored them and stepping back from the crease, he gazed up at the sky as the keeper threw the ball to mid-on who polished it briefly on his trousers, before throwing it back to the bowler.

Strickland watched as a feathery cloud passed across the face of the sun, the sky a washed-out blue. Nothing compared with a Normandy summer and he marvelled at the swifts' acrobatics, as they flew above the outfield catching insects on the wing. He looked away and saw the burly figure of Lambton facing him as the bowler turned and began to race towards the wicket once more. The man raised his arm and the ball flew like a missile towards the batsman. The bowler kept the same line and length, but this time Strickland was ready and stepping forward with his left foot he struck the ball firmly through the covers.

'Yes!' he shouted to his partner, who was already thundering down the pitch. Strickland also took off and as they passed each other, both men saw the fielder running towards the boundary. They made their first single and began another, completing the second just as the man dived and stopped the ball from crossing the rope. If they were quick they could still make one more.

'Come on!' shouted Lambton, who took off again.

Strickland knew he would have to sprint and he raced up the pitch as the fielder retrieved the ball and threw it back to the bowler, who caught it just as the batsman made it to the crease. Three runs and a chance now for the younger man to rest, while his partner took up the strike.

Lambton was an altogether different type of player to Strickland. Not for him the snatched single and a dash between the wickets. For the burly Lancastrian it was the boundary or nothing. He had only run the third because he knew it would give him the strike. Now he settled in and after calling for a mark from the umpire he took up his position, looking up at the bowler as the man prepared to make his run. Again the bowler raced towards the wicket and again he raised his arm, hurling the ball down the pitch. Lambton met the ball head on and with a well timed swing of his bat, he lofted it straight over the player's head. The ball ascended into the sky, rising ever higher until it was consumed by the sun. His partner watched and waited for it to drop, but it never did. The ball had simply vanished into the blue.

Strickland looked away and tried to make out Lambton at the other end, but he seemed indistinct, almost ethereal. There was a strange luminosity to the air, as if a golden mist had descended. The batsman could barely see his partner who was enveloped in a haze and indeed all the other players seemed to have the same spectral vagueness, as if they too had become ghosts. A wind blew and the men floated away above the ground, the air burning brighter as they did so. Strickland called out as the players drifted away like dandelion seed on the breeze, but either they could not hear him or else his voice made no difference. As they disappeared the light increased, becoming a celestial brilliance which burned ever more brightly. Such was its intensity that Strickland closed his eyes, and still the heavenly light shone and he raised a hand to his face.

The pilot awoke and found himself blinking in a shaft of sunlight, which had crept across his body as he slept. Although his limbs still hurt, the pain of the beating had diminished and he lay there quietly, realising he had been dreaming. He remembered his comrades' faces so vividly, even though they were all gone. Everyone he had served with in France was now dead, including Armstrong and Hay, the two friends who had collected him from the hospital at East Grinstead. Shortly afterwards Armstrong had ditched in the Channel and his body was never recovered. Hay became an instructor and was killed in an accident while training glider pilots for the D-Day landings. Even the indomitable Lambton was no more. Bored of a later desk job in the Air Ministry, he transferred to a Mosquito squadron and had been shot down over Holland during the battle for Arnhem. Of the squadron's original 1939 intake, only Strickland survived.

The pilot sat up and drew his knees to his chest. He looked at his wooden prison and thought it a wretched place for a man to die. Even so he accepted his fate and knew it would not be long. Today, or perhaps tomorrow. He would know soon enough. Strickland sat with his back against the bamboo wall and waited. In the distance came a steady throbbing sound. He cocked his head to one side and listened. He could hear the faint noise of a diesel engine and wondered what it was. The pilot got up and went towards the opposite wall and peering through a gap in the bamboo, he could see the grey outline of a patrol boat as it made its sluggish way across the harbour. Now he understood how the Japanese had rescued him. He watched as the boat pulled up to the jetty and the crew secured it to the wharf with ropes. The pilot could see it was a sturdy vessel, capable of crossing the roughest seas and a thought sprang into his mind. With this boat he could escape from the island. He doubted whether the Japanese would be able to follow, as he was sure it was their only means of transport. He need not travel far as he would no doubt soon be spotted by friendly aircraft patrolling the area. He could also tell them of the enemy presence on the island. The idea gave Strickland hope which lifted his spirits out of all proportion to its possibility.

The pilot went back to his corner and thought about his predicament. Plainly he must try and escape, but how? As the prisoner entertained such thoughts of freedom, he heard voices and the sound of bolts being drawn aside. The door was thrown open, revealing the two guards.

'*Shujin, tachiagaru!*' ordered one of the men, beckoning with an outstretched arm.

The Englishman stood up and the soldiers grabbed him, marching him out of the hut, across the compound and up the steps of Hayama's quarters. The captain was sitting at his desk typing a report and looked up as his prisoner appeared at the doorway, flanked by the soldiers. The guards bowed, while Strickland remained standing. He felt a sharp blow on the back of his head and one of the soldiers bellowed at him.

'*Ojigi, ohei na inu!*' ordered the soldier with his hand on the pilot's neck, forcing his head down.

'*Koko ni kinasai,*' said the captain. The guards marched the prisoner over to the captain's desk, next to which was an empty chair. Hayama motioned Strickland to take it. He sat down and the guards withdrew, but only as far as the doorway.

'Cigarette?' asked the captain, pushing a packet across the table.

'No … thank you.'

'Are you sure?'

'Yes.'

'As you wish. They're Kinshi. An excellent brand. Much better than American cigarettes,' and the Japanese officer took one from the packet and lit it, exhaling a thin cloud of smoke. He looked at his prisoner.

'Water?'

Strickland nodded and Hayama poured him a glass from a jug on the table. The pilot drank thirstily and when he had finished, he put the empty glass down.

'Thank you.'

'More?'

The pilot nodded again and his captor poured him another glass which he also drank.

'You are lucky.'

'Lucky?'

'Yes. You should have drowned. It was a miracle we found you. The currents here are strong and the sea is full of sharks.'

'Instead I am here.'

'Yes. The gods have smiled upon you.'

'I wouldn't put it that way.'

'There is no other explanation.'

The pilot observed the Japanese officer with his right eye, the left was still swollen and closed. He realised that this was going to be another interrogation session and he wondered if it would be as brutal as the first. There was silence and Hayama took a long drag on his cigarette before speaking again.

'You are stubborn. That is why you were beaten. It is much better to talk. That is all I want to do. Talk.'

Strickland continued looking at his captor with his good eye. He knew that he owed him his life, but that did not mean he was obliged to give him any information. He said nothing.

The Japanese officer returned the prisoner's gaze, observing him with all the concentration of an artist examining his subject. The man had fine features, if somewhat bloodied and beaten up. A long Grecian nose, now broken of course, thick blond hair and bright blue eyes, only one of which was visible and which remained fixed on him. He was handsome in that peculiarly English way which spoke of learning and sensibility, mixed with a residual toughness. He was sure the pilot came from a warrior caste like himself. There was a Greek word which perfectly described the man who sat before him and he tried to recall what it was. Then the captain remembered. It was 'stoic'. Hayama the naturalist could not help admiring his subject. He was a fine specimen. As an aesthete the Japanese officer appreciated the sublime and in different circumstances, he wondered how their lives might have played out. They might even have been friends. It was a pity that he had to kill him.

'So you refuse to talk?'

'That's right.'

'It would be better for you if you did.'

'I am a prisoner of war, you have obligations under the Geneva Convention of which Japan is a signatory ...'

Hayama gave his desk a resounding thump with his fist, making the empty glass jump.

'I have no obligations to you whatsoever! We are not at the League of Nations now. We are on an island in the South Pacific, which is so small and insignificant that it does not even have a name. Nobody knows you are here. No one will come looking for you. Your squadron thinks you are dead. Your family will have been informed that you are missing in action, presumed killed. As it is you are a prisoner of the Imperial Japanese Army. I am trying to conduct an interrogation in a civilised way, but you are being most disrespectful. The beating you received was entirely your fault. I have never known such insubordination. If you were in the Imperial Army you would have been executed for impudence!'

'As I'm sure you realise I am not in the Imperial Army ...'

Again the captain struck the desk, cutting Strickland short. The Japanese officer's face reddened and the pilot could see he was close to losing control.

'This is not some sort of game! I have the power of life and death over you. Do you want to die?' he asked, picking up his cigarette from the ashtray and angrily stubbing it out.

Strickland looked at him. He had already resigned himself to his fate, what did a few extra hours or days matter? It was obvious now why Hayama had saved his life. Firstly, he had wanted to stop him being rescued and thereby give away their position. Now he wanted to glean as much information as possible before killing him. If there was one thing the pilot could do before he died, it was to say nothing.

'I might owe you my life, but I do not owe you anything else. Since I did not ask to be rescued, you cannot expect me to be grateful ...'

There was a sharp blow as his captor struck him hard across the mouth with the back of his hand. Strickland reeled and felt blood trickle from his lip.

'You are insolent! Insolent in the way that you talk to me! Insolent in the way that you refuse to answer my questions! Insolent in everything!'

The pilot wiped the blood from his mouth and then spoke.

'This conversation is quite pointless. I'm not going to tell you anything other than what I am obliged to tell you under the conventions signed by our respective governments. Frustrating and inconvenient perhaps, but there it is ...'

The captain shook his head and sighed. He called out to the guards standing by the door, who had not moved at all during the two men's confrontation.

This time the pilot knew precisely what was coming as the soldiers advanced and set upon him once more, striking him about the head and shoulders and knocking him off his chair. After a time the various blows appeared to fuse together into one long, sustained beating as Strickland curled up on the floor, the guards furiously kicking and punching him. He lay there and waited, either for the beating to finish, or until he lost conciousness. Fortunately Hayama ordered the guards to stop, telling them that the prisoner had had enough and to remove him. The soldiers picked up the pilot and dragged him out of the hut and across the compound, before throwing him into the storeroom and padlocking the door once more.

Battered and bloody Strickland remained face down on the earthen floor, where the guards had left him. He did not move and lay there like a beaten animal, all sense of flight or resistance gone. He did not even have the strength to get to his knees and crawl away into a corner. Instead he lay on his side, his chest heaving with exhaustion. He ached all over, even swallowing was painful. He could barely breathe and drew air into his lungs in thin, painful rasps. Eventually the pain subsided and as it did so sleep came and drew away its sting. Strickland fell into a black pit of slumber, way beyond the realms of dreams. A pit so dark and deep that it seemed endless and still he fell further into it. He remained in that void for some time, oblivious to everything else.

A warm breeze stirred the fronds of the palms and an occasional cry came from the canopy of trees surrounding the camp as a bird burst into raucous song. Above the forest rose the mountain, a grey volcanic plug of igneous rock. A few white clouds floated above its crown like feathers in a headdress and the sky was a deep blue. The camp was quiet as the soldiers lay in their bunks sleeping, or whiled away the hours writing letters or playing cards. Music played on the gramophone and the men smiled as they listened and thought of home. The heat of the day made it pointless to venture out and even Hayama took the opportunity to rest.

The captain sat in his cabin annotating his collection of butterflies. There were scores of different varieties on the island and he was a keen entomologist. It helped fill the long periods of time between the daily reports that he made. Hayama would often go off on solitary expeditions into the forest armed only with a large butterfly net and a notebook. When he found a new specimen he would measure its wingspan, record its sex and type and sketch it. If he had not seen it before, or if it was a particularly fine example, he would take it home and add it to his collection. He picked one up in a pair of tweezers and held the lepidoptera up to the window, admiring its blue iridescent wings as they shone in the afternoon light. Just as Charles Darwin had noted with his South American finches, so the captain was convinced the surrounding islands contained several different varieties of the same species, each uniquely adapted to its own habitat. After the war he intended to donate his collection to the entomology department at his old university in Nagasaki. He was sure they would be glad to have it.

While the captain sat in his cabin admiring his butterfly collection, his prisoner began to stir from his slumber. Strickland woke to find himself in the same position on the storeroom floor. In all that time he had not even moved. He had no idea how long he had been asleep, but the light which poured through the gaps in the bamboo was burnished by the evening sun and he assumed that it must have been for some hours. Sitting up he felt his body, which was cut and bruised. His ribs ached and he prodded his sides to see if any bones had been broken. Although the flesh was tender, he could not feel any fractures. Furthermore he could still see out of his right eye, which he had managed to protect during the last assault.

The pilot realised he must act. He doubted he could survive another beating and knew he had to escape. The boat was his only chance. If he was caught, he would certainly be killed. He also knew that he would die if he did not. Either from a beating, or rotting away in the fetid darkness of his prison.

Strickland crept over to the door and peering beneath it, he could make out the boots of the soldier standing guard outside. He returned and sat down in the corner to think. He could try and get the soldier to enter the hut, but was unsure if he had the strength to overpower him. If he failed the element of surprise would be lost and the alarm would be raised. He would have to find another way. The pilot looked at the bamboo walls beside him, which seemed sturdy enough. He leant against the wood and tried to loosen the vines which bound them, but they were securely fastened. He looked up at the roof and could see that it was solid and well built. It had to be in order to keep out the monsoon rains. That meant the only other option was the floor.

The prisoner sat down on his haunches and using a discarded piece of timber, began to dig away at the foundations and was surprised to discover that although the bamboo went to a depth of a foot, the wood itself was rotten. While the poles above the ground were solid, those in the earth had been weakened by damp and bored into by beetles and were full of holes. The other buildings in the camp were raised on stilts above the ground, but the storeroom had been built into the earth to stop the rats from getting in underneath. Although the rodents had been thwarted, the wood had rotted with time. Strickland sat back against the rough palisade of bamboo and found himself smiling. He would wait until nightfall and dig himself out.

The sun set beyond a darkening sea and the day's heat was replaced by a cooler air. As dusk descended a new moon rose above the camp and the birds and monkeys in the surrounding forest fell silent. The pilot listened and waited. Everything was quiet. He crept over to the door to spy on the guard. At first he could see nothing. Then, looking to one side, he saw the soldier had slumped to the ground and was fast asleep. Strickland realised he would have to work quickly and padded across to the other wall. Using the piece of timber he began scraping at the earth, scooping it to one side until he had made a hole two feet long and over a foot deep. Room enough for him to squeeze through. With the pit dug he crept over to the door to see if the guard was still asleep and found that he was. The man snored softly, his head rising and falling on his chest.

With his heart beating quickly, Strickland returned to his work and began carefully to pull away the rotten wood. The bamboo was brittle and gave easily and soon there was an opening large enough for him to crawl through. The pilot lay down on the floor and started to inch his way through the narrow gap. Wriggling from side to side he eased his body through the hole, his shirt occasionally snagging against the bamboo, until first his head, then his shoulders and finally his torso emerged on the other side. With his upper body now free, the prisoner hauled himself out of the gap.

Strickland stayed crouched on all fours and waited in the lee of the hut, watching and listening. He could hear nothing. The camp was asleep. The air was pure and still and looking up, he could see the stars scattered in a brilliant dust across the night sky. A sliver of moon hung in the heavens and shone like a newly turned blade.

The pilot got to his feet and walked stealthily through the camp, keeping to the shadows. Beyond the trees he could see the water of the harbour glimmer like some dark stone. He headed towards the forest, his bare feet falling silently across the earth. Once he had made the line of trees he waited and looked back at the camp for the last time. The place was quiet, not even a lamp shone in the gloom.

Strickland turned and headed into the trees, making his way down the path towards the beach. The palms loomed up on either side as he slipped like a ghost between the trunks, the creepers occasionally brushing against his face as he went. As he neared the harbour he could hear the distant boom of the waves crashing against the reef. He stopped at the edge of the forest and gazed at the pale expanse of beach. It was deserted. On the other side of the ink-dark water was the pier, the patrol boat a solitary silhouette against the night sky.

The pilot left the safety of the trees and felt the cold, hard sand beneath his feet as he made his way down towards the shore. He waded into the water, its oily caress like a balm against his skin. When the water reached his waist Strickland dived under and holding his breath, he swam as far as he could before breaking the surface. His head emerged and he took a lungful of air and struck out towards the jetty. There was no noise except the gentle splash of his swimming and, farther off, the echoing reef. The pilot swam quickly, the boat looming up ahead of him. He soon made it to the pier and grasping one of the barnacled piles, he hauled himself out of the water and up onto the jetty. He saw an oil drum and hid behind it, his body dripping onto the wooden boards. He looked and waited, but there was no one about.

Strickland got to his feet, picked up the gangplank, placed it across the gunwale and boarded the boat, pulling the bridge in after him. He walked up the side and went into the wheelhouse to search for a knife and found one hanging by the radio set. He took it and swiftly cut the ropes which secured the boat. With the vessel now free, the pilot returned to start the engine. He entered the wheelhouse and searched about in the gloom for the key to the ignition box. Strickland's hands felt something smooth and metallic and holding it up, he saw he had found what he was looking for. He put the key into the lock and pressed the starter button, the boat's engines roaring into life.

The noise instantly woke the camp and the place was filled with commotion, as men ran about yelling at each other. Hayama leapt naked from his bed and realising the prisoner must have escaped, he grabbed his sword and ran out into the night, shouting at his men to stop the boat. Together with their captain the soldiers raced through the trees and across the beach towards the pier. Ahead of them they could see the vessel, its lights blazing, its engines groaning. They shouted and ran even faster as Hayama urged them on.

Inside the wheelhouse Strickland wrestled with the controls. He grabbed the throttle and never having driven a boat before, suddenly found himself reversing back along the jetty. He pushed the lever away from him and the vessel surged forward, bumping against the side of the pier as the pilot spun the wheel with his other hand. He was oblivious to everything else as he desperately tried to get the boat away from the pier, the propellers madly churning the water. So he did not see the soldiers sprinting towards him or even hear them jump aboard. The last thing that Strickland knew was an explosion inside his head like a flashbulb and as the pulsing light diminished in waves, a giant black flower enveloped him in an embrace. The pilot's body lay slumped unconscious on the wheelhouse floor, a soldier standing over him with a wrench in his hand.

FOUR

Hayama sat in his hut sharpening his sword. He rubbed the blade against the whetstone in long, even strokes, turning it from side to side, his hands working up and down making the bright metal gleam. He took a cloth and wiped the blade clean and holding the weapon up to the light, he watched its edge glint in the morning sun. The captain was the fourteenth generation of his family to own the weapon and he took as much care of it as a mother did her newborn child. He even talked and sang to it. With the newly polished sword flashing in his hand, Hayama began to recite an old martial song.

> *Across the sea, corpses in the water;*
> *Across the mountain, corpses in the field.*
> *I shall die only for the Emperor,*
> *I shall never look back.*

He stopped singing and leaning forward, he tenderly kissed the blade. Together with his family the captain loved this sword more than anything else in the world. In fact, the notion of sword and family were not separate entities for a samurai, but united like the magnolia and its flower. The tree nourished the flower and the flower propagated the tree. Hayama had never had the opportunity to use the sword before. Now he did. The captain put his weapon back into its scabbard and stood up. It was time to execute the Englishman.

Hayama put on his forage cap and went outside. The midday sun flared like a match in the sky, its light momentarily blinding him and he pulled the cap further over his eyes. The company was lined up opposite and when they saw their captain appear, Noguchi gave an order and the men snapped to attention. The senior NCO saluted his officer and Hayama returned the greeting. The captain stood on the verandah facing his men, his sword hanging by his side.

'Sergeant Noguchi,' he said. 'Bring me the prisoner.'

'*Heitai-san*,' replied the subordinate and turning, he repeated the order to two of his men.

The soldiers marched over to a corrugated iron box on the edge of the compound and slid back the bolts. They dragged the pilot out and brought him before their captain, forcing him to kneel before returning to the ranks.

The prisoner was in a wretched state; his blond hair was matted with blood, his shirt was torn at the shoulder and his hands were tightly bound. Standing and watching along with the other soldiers was Hayama's orderly Ito. He looked at the man crouching on the ground in front of the captain and felt sorry for him. The orderly knew he was the enemy and that he had tried to escape. He also knew it was wrong to kill a man in cold blood. It was not honourable. He wanted to say something, to tell the captain that what he was about to do was a crime, but he was too frightened to speak out. Instead he began to pray.

Strickland knelt there in the dust, knowing his final hour had come. He did not look up. Instead he kept his head down and stared at the grit between his fingers. It would be the last thing he would ever see. He was ready to die and he hoped his executioner would be quick.

The captain descended the steps and addressed his men.

'I humbly make this sacrifice to the God Emperor. May the spilling of our enemy's blood please his Imperial Majesty!'

Hayama stood over the pilot and placing both his hands upon the hilt, he unsheathed the sword and raised it above his head. Beneath him lay the bare nape of the Englishman's neck. A single blow and the man's severed head would fall from his shoulders.

He stood there with his sword held high in the sun and prepared to bring it down upon his enemy's neck. It would all be over in a moment. The captain remained poised but the sword, which had always been so light and easy to use, seemed to hang like a dead weight in his hands. As the Japanese officer held the sword above his head, the weapon became heavier and he felt himself sweating beneath the hot sun. He gripped the hilt more tightly and the sword began to shake in his grasp. The men stood silently watching their captain, waiting for him to despatch the Englishman. Yet the moment would not come. Instead Hayama stood there petrified like a statue. Sweat poured down his face and dripped off the end of his chin, as he clasped the weapon above his head. The men waited and held their breath. The sun circled the heavens and the earth stood still. Finally the captain lowered the sword and replaced it in its scabbard. Without a word he turned on his heel and strode back to his cabin.

The soldiers remained motionless until Noguchi stepped forward and dismissed them with a shout. He took the pilot by the scruff of his neck and hauled him back to the punishment box, shoving him inside with his boot before slamming the door shut and sliding the bolts across. The sergeant gave the tin box a resounding kick and cursing the prisoner, he walked away.

Inside the tiny cell it was unbearably hot. The pilot sat there, his clothes soaked in sweat, hardly able to believe he was still alive. Had Hayama meant to kill him, or had he been subject to a mock execution?

Perhaps the captain had lost his nerve? Whatever it was, it did not change his predicament, he was still a prisoner. He put a hand to the back of his head and tenderly felt the bruise at the base of his skull. His vision was still blurred and he was fortunate the blow he received on the boat had not broken his neck. Strickland removed his hand and looked up. There was a narrow slit between the door and roof through which he could see the camp, the ground white in the morning sun. He wondered how much longer he could survive like this. The pilot thought it would not be too long, a couple of days perhaps. He had so nearly escaped but it did not matter, he would die here.

The sun beat down mercilessly as the pilot sat alone in the punishment box, hunched up like an animal as he contemplated his last remaining hours. He would end his days incarcerated in an enemy camp on a remote tropical island beneath the burning sky, far away from home. His parents would never know what became of him and they would have no grave to mourn. He might end up as a name on some war memorial. When they died his memory would perish with them and he would be forgotten. There would be nothing left of his life, just his bones dissolving into this dry earth. Man, for all his toil and struggle, was merely dust.

Strickland closed his eyes and tried to rest. He dozed fitfully for the remainder of the day, as afternoon turned into evening and the sun disappeared behind the tops of the trees. A long shadow fell across the camp and the moon rose into the sky, as the evening brought cooler air. Inside the box the pilot stirred, his consciousness raised by the drop in the temperature. He did not wake fully and remained in a corner with his eyes closed, his body racked by dehydration. His tongue felt like a piece of boiled meat and he could barely swallow. The camp was quiet except for an occasional cry from a monkey, as the troop settled down for the night. As darkness fell a shard of moon shone and the constellations appeared one by one, their lights strung out across the heavens like fishermen's lamps.

The pilot remained curled up inside the punishment box, his eyes closed, his arms around his knees, the cords that bound him cutting into his wrists. A sound came from outside and he thought that it must be the rats scavenging in the dust. Then he heard a voice whispering. Strickland opened his eyes and saw a water bottle being passed through the slit above the door, together with a few slices of coconut. He took the bottle with both hands and opening it he drank its contents, slaking his thirst. When he had finished he handed the bottle back, whispering his gratitude.

'*Kirisuto-kyoto*,' said the voice. '*Kirisuto-kyoto.*'

Strickland did not understand, but he knew that whoever the man was, he had saved his life.

'Thank you, thank you,' he murmured.

'God bless!' said his companion and with that his saviour was gone. Wide awake and refreshed the pilot picked up the slices of coconut from the floor and began to eat them. They were sweet and tender and he thought that he had never tasted anything so delicious. It was extraordinary what a little sustenance could do to raise a man's spirits. One of the soldiers in the camp must have taken pity on him, although he had no idea who it was. The man was certainly brave as he knew that if Hayama ever found out, he would kill him. Strickland wondered what it was the man had been saying to him and he berated himself for not knowing any Japanese. He had also said 'God bless!' in English. What on earth did he mean? Plainly not everyone on the island was as brutal as the captain. Then he wondered if the man's kindness was perhaps a trick. A plan by Hayama to beguile him and get him to talk. Yet the more the pilot thought about it, the more he felt it unlikely. The captain must have known by now that he would not talk and such a ruse would be pointless.

Strickland finished the slices of coconut and satisfied, he sat back. He felt much better, but the act of charity also created another problem. Since no one in his position would ever refuse food and drink, the pilot realised he could survive inside the box almost indefinitely. Perhaps he could persuade his new friend to help him escape again. If he did he would have to take the man with him. He could not leave him here for Hayama to discover. Strickland did not know what to do and hoped that his mysterious helper might have a solution. With these thoughts in his mind, he laid his head against the corrugated walls of his tin cell and in a short while fell asleep. Outside, the camp was steeped in silence, the trees a solid mass. Nothing moved or called out in the stillness. In the sky stars flickered and burned and the crescent moon shone.

For three days and nights the pilot languished in the punishment box. The hut reeked of urine and sweat and during the day the temperature would make him faint. Then every night his secret friend would bring water and slices of coconut, always adding a few words of encouragement in English. Occasionally Hayama would come and bang on the roof, demanding that he talk and each time Strickland would remain silent so that the captain would rage and shout, before storming back to his quarters.

After nightfall the pilot would wait patiently for his companion and when he arrived, he would try and engage him in conversation. The soldier spoke good if accented English, but he was obviously frightened and kept telling him to be quiet and just to eat. Then he would disappear and Strickland would be left alone again.

In the long hours of darkness he prayed, remembering a Spanish friar who had once been in a similar predicament. In the sixteenth century a man called Juan de Yepes, better known as John of the Cross, had been incarcerated for his ascetic beliefs, which were too radical for the church at the time. Rather than being downhearted, the friar had been inspired by his solitude. Eventually, Fray Juan escaped from his prison with the help of a friendly gaoler and used the experience to his advantage, establishing a religious order of his own. Taking comfort from this, Strickland refused to give up. Outside it was dark and so too was the pilot's soul within. But his unknown provider had kindled a small flame of hope, which nourished him just as much as food and water.

On the fourth day of the pilot's incarceration Hayama was sitting alone in his hut, deep in contemplation. He had had enough. The prisoner must be super human, either that or he was blessed by the gods. He should have been dead by now. Instead he was just as insolent as ever. Of course, Hayama had no idea the pilot had a secret provider and if he had he would, as Strickland had so rightly guessed, have killed him. But the

Japanese officer did not know and he just did not understand. By keeping him in the punishment box, he had hoped to break the prisoner's spirit. Yet, if anything the man seemed to be getting stronger. The captain knew that it could not go on like this, he was beginning to look foolish. Either he executed the Englishman, or he released him. Since he knew he was unable to do the former, it would have to be the latter.

The captain got up and went to the door. He looked and saw a solitary soldier sweeping the compound. He called out and told the man to stop what he was doing and to go and fetch Sergeant Noguchi. The man ran off and the barrel-chested NCO soon appeared, bowing at his commanding officer. Hayama told him he had decided to release the prisoner and that he should inform the men. If the sergeant was surprised at the captain's decision he did not show it, and simply bowed his head again.

'Mr Strickland is also an officer and as my guest he is to be treated accordingly,' added the captain. 'Any man who fails to show him proper respect will be severely punished.'

The sergeant required no further explanation and bowing once more, he went off to inform the men of the captain's order.

Hayama watched as Noguchi walked across the compound and disappeared into the other ranks' quarters. He had made his decision and he raised his eyes to heaven and asked the gods to give him strength. The captain steeled himself and breathing deeply, he descended the wooden steps of his hut and walked out into the midday glare. The sun bore down upon the camp, chasing the shadows into the corners. The surrounding trees seemed to wilt in the heat, not a breath of wind stirred their leaves. Even the monkeys lay silently in the canopies, conserving their energy. The only noise was the incessant scream of the cicadas, the air vibrating in waves to their constant rhythm. The cacophany rang madly in the captain's ears, as he walked across the compound towards the punishment box. Still the cicadas sang, their voices shaking the trees. Hayama ignored the torrent of noise and going up to the corrugated box, he slid the bolts across and opened the door. The smell inside was rancid and instinctively he drew back.

'Follow me,' the captain said and without another word he walked away.

Strickland sat on the floor, his arms covering his eyes, the light blinding him. He blinked, unaccustomed to the glare and removing his limbs from his face, he saw the khaki figure of Hayama climbing the steps of his hut and disappearing inside. What on earth did he want now? Was he going to get another beating? Or worse? The only way to find out was to follow him and so the pilot crawled out of the punishment box and got groggily to his feet. The heat and the burning sun made his head swim and shielding his eyes again, he staggered across the compound to Hayama's quarters expecting one last interrogation session.

Strickland entered the hut and saw the captain sitting at his desk, the light from the window glancing across his body, leaving his face in shadow. He looked at the prisoner and beckoned him forward.

'Please,' he said, indicating the empty chair.

The pilot shuffled over towards the desk and sat down.

'Cigarette?' asked the captain, offering the packet.

Strickland hesitated briefly before accepting one and Hayama produced his lighter and lit it for him. Then he took one for himself and lit that too. He sat there for a while puffing away, not saying anything, the tobacco smoke ascending the shaft of sunlight that streamed through the open shutters. The pilot watched and smoked, wondering what was going to happen. Finally, the captain spoke.

'I have decided to release you.'

The pilot was stunned, although he continued to draw on his cigarette as if what Hayama had just said was perfectly natural.

'Of course you cannot leave this island. But you are free to go wherever you like.'

Strickland did not reply and simply exhaled, filling the air with tobacco smoke. He was trying to work things out. Why was Hayama releasing him when he had told him many times that he was going to die? Why did he not just kill him? The more the pilot thought about it, the more it did not make any sense. Perhaps the Japanese officer was psychotic and was simply playing games with him before he executed him.

'I'm sorry … I don't understand …'

'I have no choice. I cannot kill you, so I must let you go.'

The pilot sat there looking perplexed.

'If you don't want to kill me, you don't have to release me either.'

The captain sighed and flicked the glowing tip of his cigarette into the ashtray.

'I know. But whether you are inside the punishment box or here on the island, you are still under my command. I have simply decided to grant you your freedom. The island is yours to wander wherever you wish. However, I do have one request.'

'And what is that?'

'That you do not try and escape again.'

Strickland took a final drag of his cigarette, and extinguished it. The captain's demand seemed reasonable. He knew the only way off the island was the boat and he doubted the ignition key would be left in the wheelhouse again.

'Fine,' he said.

Hearing this Hayama visibily relaxed and leant back in his chair and stubbed out his cigarette in the ashtray, the butt glowing briefly before dying in a final curl of smoke. He opened a drawer in his desk and pulled out a small knife. Strickland's brow furrowed, but he need not have worried as the captain took hold of the pilot's hands and cut the cords.

'Thank you,' he said, rubbing his wrists.

'You must be thirsty. Would you like something to drink?'

'Yes, please.'

The captain called out and his orderly appeared silently at his shoulder, like a genie that could be summoned at will. His commanding officer asked him to bring them some tea and

bowing, the man disappeared. Behind the screen, which separated the kitchen from Hayama's living quarters, came a clatter
as a kettle was pulled off the stove, followed by a clink of por-
celain as a pot was filled and cups were gathered. Ito presently
reappeared carrying the tea on a tray. He set it down in front of
the captain and without meeting his eyes, he bowed and went
away again.

Hayama leant forward, picked up the teapot and began
to pour. He raised his cup and smiled at Strickland. The pilot
lifted his own cup and beyond its rim, he could see the captain's smiling face. He returned the look before sipping his tea.
It was scalding and sweet and delicately scented and Strickland,
having spent four days in the punishment box surviving on a
diet of coconut and water, thought he had never tasted anything
so delicious. The tea revived and invigorated him. He finished
his cup and put it down on the table.

'Some more?' asked Hayama, his hand on the pot. The pilot
nodded and the captain poured him another cup. This time
Strickland drank it slowly, savouring its aroma. Although he
enjoyed the tea, there was something else which troubled him
and he wondered if he should ask the captain. His captor seemed
calm and he thought that he would not mind.

'I'm still curious as to why you rescued me.'

The Japanese officer refreshed his own cup and took a sip,
then put it down again. He looked directly at Strickland as he
answered, his dark eyes upon him.

'To be honest I wasn't going to, but you sent out a distress
flare, which meant that you must have survived the crash. I had
to look for you. If you had been picked up by your own side or
by the Americans, you would have given away our position.'

'I didn't know there was anybody on the island.'

'I couldn't be sure of that. And besides if you had been rescued
your superiors would have drawn their own conclusions. How
was it that our submarines could remain at sea for months on
end, without being replenished in port? At the very least they

would need food and fresh water. There had to be other bases in the South Pacific.'

The pilot smiled at the thought of an enemy soldier saving his life in order to preserve his own and was certain he would have done the same. The irony was that had he known there were Japanese on the island, he would never have sent the distress flare.

'Do your superiors know about me?'

'No.'

'Why not?'

The captain looked down at his cup and ran his finger around the rim. Plainly he had asked himself the same quesiton.

'I don't know. At first I thought you were going to die, so it didn't matter. And now ...' the captain's voice trailed off and he simply shrugged. He looked up and saw the pilot's scarred hands, which held his cup. The skin was thick and discoloured like meat that has been left out in the sun, while the index and middle finger on the left hand were fused together.

'What happened?' he asked, indicating the pilot's hands.

Strickland studied them, as if he had only just noticed.

'I was shot down ...'

'Where?'

'In England. I was attacked by a Messerschmitt. It was entirely my fault.'

'Your plane caught fire?'

The pilot nodded, the memory of his escape from his burning aircraft still vivid.

'You're lucky to be alive.'

'Yes, I am. I spent six months in hospital.'

'The doctors must have been skilled.'

'They were. It was only because of them that I survived.'

'And they let you fly again?'

Strickland shook his head and took another swig of tea.

'Not at first. To begin with I was grounded and could only do observational duties. But I wanted to fly and eventually my commanding officer relented.'

'Why did you want to fly again?'

'I wanted to fight. We were short of pilots and I hated being on the ground, while my friends were being killed in the air.'

Hayama nodded and noticed the purple and white ribbon above the pilot's breast pocket.

'Is that a decoration?'

'Yes, it is. It's a DFC.'

Hayama raised his eyebrows briefly.

'A Distinguished Flying Cross. It's a gallantry medal. I didn't actually deserve it. They gave it to me because of my wounds. I wasn't expected to be airborne again.'

'You must be very determined.'

'Stubborn, perhaps.'

'You tried to swim to the island.'

'I didn't get very far.'

'It would have been impossible. The current is too strong. You should have drowned.'

The pilot smiled laconically and drank his tea.

'I did try.'

The captain looked quizically at him, not understanding at first. Then he realised it was a joke and he too smiled.

'I'm sorry I saved your life.'

'There's always a reason.'

Hayama stopped smiling and looked directly at Strickland.

'Yes, there is,' he said. 'There is a reason for everything. Everything under heaven.'

'And that is why we are here?'

Hayama did not answer but studied the pilot with a fierce intensity, his energy pent up inside him as if he were an animal about to seize its prey. For a moment Strickland thought the captain was going to strike him. Instead he put the tea tray to one side and pushed his chair back.

'Come with me,' he said, rising to his feet.

Strickland got up and watched as the captain marched out of his hut and descending the steps, he went over to an adjacent building and disappeared inside. The pilot followed and entered the hut behind him. The place was similar to Hayama's quarters although not quite as spacious and there was no kitchen at the back. It was dry and well kept, with a bed in one corner, together with a table and chair and a rack of shelves against one wall.

'This is where you will sleep,' announced Hayama. 'You will dine in my quarters with me. I have already informed the men that I have released you and they are to treat you according to your rank, regardless of the fact that you are the enemy. I have also told them you are my guest and that you are answerable only to me.'

The pilot merely nodded as he surveyed his new quarters, it was certainly better than the punishment box. On one of the shelves was a framed photograph of a young Japanese officer in uniform. Strickland picked it up, wiping the dust from the glass.

'Who's this?' he asked, as he held the picture towards the captain.

'His name is Shinzo Aoki. He was my second in command. He was a naval ensign and responsible for the patrol boat. He died of a fever. These were his quarters.'

'I'm sorry,' said the pilot and he replaced the photograph back on the shelf.

'I suggest you rest now and return to my quarters for supper. You should have everything you need here. There is a shower outside if you want to wash.'

Strickland knew that he must stink after his incarceration and was grateful for the opportunity to purge the grime from his body.

'I'm afraid I do not have a spare razor, but if you wish to shave you can borrow mine.'

The pilot rubbed a hand across his jaw which now showed the beginnings of a beard, the hair wiry and blond. The shave could wait, although he certainly needed a shower.

'Thank you,' he replied and before he could say anything else Hayama turned and, without another word, left the hut.

Strickland remained alone in the room, with only the ghost of a naval lieutenant for company. He hoped the previous occupant would not be too concerned that an enemy pilot was using his quarters and would not haunt him. There was a door at the back of the hut and he opened it, stepping outside onto a small verandah. He descended the steps and beneath the eave was the shower Hayama had mentioned. It consisted of no more than a rainwater butt and a chain to release its contents.

The pilot stripped off his clothes and laid them over the rail and stood there naked, the bucket hanging above his head. He pulled the chain and felt the tepid water sluice down his body. He then picked up a bar of soap and lathered himself all over. When he had scrubbed his body from head to toe he tugged at the chain again, letting the water cascade over him until he had rinsed the soap away, the suds running off his limbs and soaking the dusty earth. For the first time in days Strickland felt what it was to be human again, all the degradation and filth of his confinement lying in a soapy pool at his feet. He stepped out from under the shower and dried himself with his hands and put his clothes back on. After he had dressed, the pilot climbed up the steps and went back inside the hut.

The wash refreshed Strickland, but his recent ordeal had also left him exhausted and he went over to the bed to rest. He removed his dog tags from around his neck and placed them on the shelf next to the picture of Ensign Aoki. He took off his shirt and drew aside the mosquito net, lying down on the thin mattress. His head on the pillow, he stared up at the wooden rafters. In the corner above him a pale gecko hung upside down on a beam, its head cocked as it listened for an unsuspecting insect to come its way. Strickland watched as it suddenly scuttled across the wood, evidently sensing something before stopping again. It hung there poised and perfectly still, its amber irises reflecting the afternoon light as it waited for its prey. The pilot closed his eyes. The bed was comfortable and soon tiredness overwhelmed him and he drifted off, watched over by the ever vigilant gecko.

Shaded by the forest the room was dim and cool and Strickland fell into a deep slumber. Outside the cicadas screamed incessantly and the sun burned a hole in the sky.

The captain sat at his desk typing his daily report. It contained the usual material about enemy activity in the area of which there had been plenty recently. They had spotted two American destroyers that day and his lookout had carefully plotted their speed and course. He hoped I-47 was still in the vicinity and that she would be able to continue her endeavors against the enemy. There was one fact in particular which Hayama had failed to mention in his report and which would have been of considerable interest to his superiors in Osaka. And that was the presence on the island of an RAF pilot. Yet the captain continued to keep that information to himself and neither he, nor anybody else, knew why.

Hayama stopped his typing and leaning back in his chair, he lit a cigarette. There was something else which troubled him, even though he knew his decision to release the pilot had been correct. There was a risk, albeit a small one, that his superiors would find out. It was true they were isolated and out of contact with other Japanese forces, but what if a submarine appeared unnannounced? It was unlikely, there were not many left in the vicinity and they always had advance notice. But it was possible a vessel might arrive in the middle of the night as they slept and discover that he had an enemy aviator in his hands. What then? The commander would certainly report it and Hayama would be questioned. Why had he not mentioned this before? He would be court martialled and probably executed for treason. His family would be disgraced and his father would commit *seppuku*.

The captain knew only that his fate lay with the gods. He placed his cigarette in the ashtray and continued writing his report, occasionally taking a drag, then finally stubbing it out. When he had finished he tore the paper from the typewriter, put on his cap and left his quarters. With the missive in his hand, he wandered through the forest and walked up over the escarpment, whistling as he went. Hayama trotted down the narrow path that led to the signals hut, keeping away from the cliff edge where the sea crashed and boiled in a cauldron below. The contrast between the north and the south of the island fascinated him. Here the country was wild and rugged. There was no protection from the winds and nor was there any reef, so that it felt the full force of the sea which pounded the rocky coast. The palms that grew were not tall and graceful as on the leeward side, but bent and stunted and clung precariously to the soil. There were no monkeys here either, only birds. A colony of terns nested on the sheer cliff face, their white forms forever wheeling and screaming above the echoing surf.

The commanding officer entered the hut and greeted his signallers, who rose to their feet and bowed. Both men had recently been informed of the prisoner's release. But if either Corporal Higa or Private Kamiko questioned the wisdom of the decision, they did not show it. If the captain chose to be merciful, so be it.

The signallers got to work and patched in the appropriate leads before dialling up the connection, while Hayama put on a set of headphones and waited until it was time to broadcast his report. On the hour the captain began to read, Higa diligently tapping out the words with the morse key using their own special code and within a couple of minutes the process was complete. Hayama thanked his signallers and removing the headphones, he told them that there would be an extra jar of *sake* for everyone that night. The soldiers were grateful, alcohol and cigarettes were strictly rationed and each man was careful to conserve his own supply. The captain got up and the signallers both rose and bowed again, expressing their thanks.

The commanding officer left the radio shack and walking back down the escarpment, he made his way to the shrine. Since the pilot's arrival, the past few days had been difficult for Hayama and he had constantly asked his ancestors who had gone before him to illuminate his path. When he got to the shrine the captain removed his cap and began to light some incense sticks and candles. As the incense sticks smouldered, he stood in front of the Buddha and reverently lowered his head.

Hayama prayed for his family and for the men under his command. They were also like family to him. He loved them all equally. He felt as if he were a father to his men. He cherished each of them as his own son, yet he also had to show them discipline. A father who failed in that would never be respected by his children. He also prayed for the pilot whom he had just released. He did not know why he had done this and he could not explain it, but he felt that his ancestors had guided him in his decision. The captain stood there deep in contemplation, his head bowed before his god. The gilded Buddha looked on, smiling serenely, impervious to the vicissitudes of the temporal world. There was no beginning and no end, just the constant turning of the great wheel. Nothing ever changed, not even change itself. All was vanity. Reality itself was a dream. Man was no more than a bubble on the ocean of nothingness. A solitary finger pointing at the moon.

The captain finished praying and replacing his cap, he bowed once more and left the shrine, making his way back through the forest towards the camp. He took the path that led through the trees and walked across the white beach, his boots slipping in the sand. The evening sun descended beyond the reef, leaving a crimson stain on a darkening sea. The captain did not stop and carried on up the path towards the camp. Shadows fell across the compound and the windows of the huts were lit by lamps. From the men's quarters an accordion played. Hayama continued on, passing the pilot's dwelling before reaching his own.

He walked up the steps and entered his quarters. Once inside he went over to his bed and changed out of his uniform and into his kimono. It was a ritual he performed every evening and one which helped him forget about the war, if only for a while. He tied the cord of his silk gown and picking up his violin he sat down on the tatami and began to play, singing softly to himself. He recited a poem written many centuries before by a monarch praising the beauty of his kingdom.

> *Countless are the mountains in Yamato,*
> *But perfect is the heavenly hill of Kagu;*
> *When I climb it and survey my realm,*
> *Over the wide plains the smoke wreaths rise and rise,*
> *Over the wide lake the gulls are on the wing;*
> *A beautiful land it is, the Land of Yamato!*

Lying on his bed, Strickland was woken by a curious sound and thought that a mosquito must be tormenting him. He opened his eyes and heard a man singing, accompanied by an unearthly tune. It seemed to come from Hayama's quarters and the pilot drew aside the muslin curtain and went over to the window. He opened the shutters and stood and listened. An ethereal music drifted in on the breeze, the notes of the violin rising and falling with the captain's voice. Strickland stood at the window, spellbound. The music stopped, but the notes lingered in the evening air like perfume, eventually dissipating in the dusk.

The pilot put on his shirt and leaving his quarters, he walked over to the captain's hut. He ascended the wooden steps, pushed open the fly screen and stepped inside. Hayama was sitting cross-legged before him, the violin to one side. He looked up as the Englishman entered.

'Good evening,' he said. 'Did you sleep well?'

'Yes, thank you. I heard you playing.'

'I'm sorry if I disturbed you.'

'No, it was beautiful. What was it?'

'Just a simple song. It reminds me of home,' Hayama replied, a wistful note in his voice.

The captain motioned for Strickland to join him on the tatami. The pilot came and sat down, crossing his legs and finding the rush matting surprisingly comfortable.

'Ito is just preparing our supper. He won't be long. Would you like some *sake* while we wait?'

'Yes, thank you,' replied his guest and Hayama called out to his orderly to bring them some rice wine.

In a moment Ito apperead, carrying a steaming jug and two small cups on a tray. He set down the jug and cups next to the captain, his mop of dark hair falling over his face as he did so. The pilot noticed his youth and knew that although Asians often appeared younger than they were, the man must be at least in his mid-twenties. They were probably the same age, but the orderly looked as if he had only just left school. His face was smooth, almost feminine, with only a trace of fine hair on his upper lip. There was a feline quality to him, even his eyes were like a cat's. Ito asked the captain if he wanted anything else, but his superior shook his head and the orderly disappeared into the kitchen. Hayama poured Strickland some *sake* before replacing the jug in its holder. The pilot took the cup and drank, the hot sweet wine warming his throat. Then he realised that the captain had failed to fill his own cup.

'Are you not having any?'

The captain smiled. Of course the Englishman would not know the form.

'In company you cannot fill your own cup with *sake*. It must be done by someone else.'

'Sorry,' said Strickland and he picked up the jug and poured a measure for his host.

'*Domo arigato*,' replied Hayama and seeing that the pilot did not understand he explained. 'It's Japanese for thank you.'

Chastened, his guest repeated the word.

'*Subarashii!*' said his host smiling, 'which means "wonderful". You'll be speaking Japanese in no time.'

Strickland looked bashful, he was ashamed he did not have even the simplest understanding of the language. All he knew were the various types of aircraft, naval vessels and military equipment that Japan possessed. He wondered where Hayama had learned his English, which he spoke fluently and with only the trace of an accent.

'Your English is excellent.'

'I lived in Honolulu. I spent three years in Oahu as part of a military exchange programme. It's a wonderful island. The country is full of butterflies, there are countless varieties and some of them haven't even been recorded.'

Strickland looked around the room and saw the lepidoptera which Hayama had caught and placed in frames along the wall, their azure wings glinting like scales in the lamplight.

'Are butterflies your passion?'

'Yes. But not just butterflies. I love all insects. They are perfectly evolved for whatever it is they are designed to do. They are born, they procreate, they die. If only mankind were as efficient.'

The pilot turned his gaze from the collection and faced the captain.

'What were you doing in Hawaii?'

'I was a military attaché.'

'Were you spying?'

Hayama gave Strickland an enigmatic look.

'Let's just say that I was watching them and they were watching me. Besides my American counterpart was based in Okinawa and I don't think he was there to play baseball.'

The pilot saw his host's cup was empty and refilled it. Hayama grinned and returned the compliment. Strickland felt emboldened by the wine and his host's conviviality and decided to ask him something that he had often put to his colleagues, but no one seemed to know the answer. Or if they thought they did, he found their explanation unsatisfactory.

'Forgive me if I sound impertinent. I have always wondered why Japan attacked Pearl Harbor. What was the point of starting a war with the United States?'

The captain sighed and raising his cup to his lips he knocked back the contents, and put it down again. Strickland picked up the jug and replenished it and the captain took another sip before replying.

'It is most unfortunate. In the end we had no choice. The Americans were determined to have a war with Japan. Not President Roosevelt and Ambassador Grew. I think they were honest and truly did not seek conflict. But there were others like Cordell Hull, who wanted war. They made so many demands upon the Motherland that it was impossible to accommodate them, without suffering a severe loss of face. When an enemy is determined to strike, you must strike him first.'

'So why did Japan become allied with the Axis?'

'That was a terrible mistake. Our traditional enemies are China and Russia. We had treaties with both before we tore them up. The problem with Japan is that we are a small nation surrounded by three very powerful ones. To the north is Russia, to the west is China and to the east is America. It makes us nervous. We always think that our neighbours want to attack us.'

There was a noise from behind the screen and looking up the pilot saw Ito emerge, carrying a tray. The officers watched as the orderly set it down on the low table next to them and began to place the various bowls and dishes on it. There was a bamboo pot of boiled rice, a plate of sea urchins with their shells split open, their yellow flesh glistening against the dark spines, a bowl of dried seaweed, another of bean sprouts, one of baked aubergine and finally a plate which contained a single grilled mullet, its head and tail attached.

'You spoil us, Ito,' said Hayama, looking at the spread which lay before them.

'It is only simple food, sir,' replied the orderly, bowing his head.

As the captain and his cook chatted together, Strickland listened. There was something in the cadence of the orderly's voice which he recognised. He was certain of it. It had the same timbre, the same gentle, fluting notes. The pilot suddenly realised the voice belonged to the man who had come in the dead of night and given him sustenance while he was in the punishment box. But he knew he should not mention it.

Ito left and Hayama urged his guest to eat. Together they began to serve themselves, starting with the sea urchins which they ate with chopsticks, dipping the flesh into a small bowl of soy sauce.

'Your orderly is a wonderful cook, where is he from?' asked the pilot, wanting to learn more about the mysterious servant.

'He's from Nagasaki like me, which is why I chose him as my orderly. He's also brilliant at catching fish. It must be something in his blood, he comes from a long line of fishermen. His family are Christian. He went to a Jesuit missionary school. He also speaks good English.'

Strickland smiled inwardly, his host unaware that he knew this much about his servant. He put his chopsticks into the pot of rice, picking up a lump which he dipped in plum sauce.

'Is Christianity common in Japan?'

'Not particularly, but Nagasaki is the most westernised part of the country. The Portuguese came in the sixteenth century and evangelised much of the area. In return for allowing the Jesuits to convert the local population, the *daimyos* were able to trade with the Portuguese. Spices and silk from Macau in exchange for silver and steel from Kyoto. However, things were not always easy, occasionally a ruler would be overthrown and another would take his place and slaughter the Christians. One ruler, Toyotomi Hideyoshi, attacked the missions, believing they threatened his authority.'

'What happened?'

'He crucified twenty-six Christians on Nishizaka hill in Nagasaki. Even so, they were never wiped out entirely and the shoguns came to realise that trade was more important than pogroms and the monasteries and churches were rebuilt. Unfortunately that only lasted for a time. Later rulers brutally purged the city of Christians and this caused the Shimabara rebellion ...'

Hayama paused and adjusted his position on the tatami as his guest looked on.

'Tell me more.'

'Well, it was very bloody. Nearly 40,000 people including 15,000 warriors barricaded themsleves inside Hara Castle. They held out for ten weeks until they were finally crushed. The leaders were decapitated and their heads put on spikes along Dejima bridge, before they were buried next to the graves of the twenty-six martyrs.'

Strickland nodded and dipped his chopsticks into the bowl of bean sprouts and took a portion.

'Did Chistianity spread across all Japan?'

'Only briefly. The sixteenth century was what we call the Christian century, after that rulers decided that any contact with foreigners diluted Japanese society. The missionaries were seen as being largely responsible for this and both they and their converts were persecuted. It was only when Japan was opened up by Commodore Perry and his 'black ships' that Christianity flourished again. But it has always had its roots in Nagasaki.'

'I see,' said the Englishman.

Strickland understood now why Ito had risked his life to help him. His natural antipathy towards a foreigner and an enemy being subsumed by his faith. The pilot realised that he owed his life to the orderly, just as much as he did to Hayama.

'And what about you? Where are you from?' asked the captain, helping himself to some aubergine before sprinkling a little dried seaweed on it.

'Northumberland. It's in the north-east of England. There are a lot of Christians there too.'

The captain smiled, he enjoyed the Englishman's sense of humour.

'But not many Buddhists?'

'I'm afraid not.'

'And your family? Do you have brothers and sisters?'

'No, there's just me.'

Hayama said nothing and they continued to eat for a while in silence. The captain was glad he had not taken the life of a mother's only son. For whatever reason the gods had stayed his hand and he knew they had been right to do so.

'Tell me a bit more about yourself,' said the captain.

'What do you want to know?'

'I don't know. Anything. Why did you become a pilot?'

'I knew there was going to be a war, so I joined the university air squadron.'

'Where were you at university?'

'Oxford. But I was only there for a year. When the war came I was called up into the RAF. We were trained in Scotland before being sent to France.'

'And after that you were shot down.'

'Yes, during the Battle of Britain.'

'Ah, I remember your Winston Churchill talking about "The Few". He is greatly respected in Japan.'

'Why is that?'

'He is from a noble family and he served and fought as a soldier before becoming a politician. It is the best way. It is how Japan is governed. The army carries out the Emperor's will.'

'And your Emperor is a god?'

'Yes. We have many deities and he is one of them. The difference is that the Emperor is living on this earth.'

'So the war is his will?'

'It is the will of all Japan. It is a struggle for national survival.'

'And if you lose this war?'

Hayama stopped eating and putting his chopsticks down, he looked at Strickland as if what he had just said was not only absurd, but impossible.

'Japan cannot lose this war, because Japan will never surrender.'

'So the war will go on forever.'

'No war goes on forever. One day there will be peace.'

'Then we can all go home.'

The captain gave a melancholy smile. He had not been home for four years. He would love to go home and see his parents. He wondered how much they had changed. His father would probably be a little greyer and a bit more stooped, but his mother would doubtless be the same. Always fussing over him, making sure he had this and that and preparing his favourite dishes. How his heart ached to go home.

Hayama looked at the table in front of them. The food had all been eaten and the *sake* was cold. The lamps in the hut burned low and stifling a yawn with his hand, the captain suggested they turn in.

The pilot got to his feet and thanking his host he left the hut, feeling sated and slightly drunk. He stepped outside into the cool night air and looked up at the heavens. A shooting star cast a pale streak across the sky, disappearing into the abyss. Strickland saw it as a good omen and made a wish. The pilot continued staring up at the constellations littering the heavens, until finally he turned away. He ascended the steps of his cabin and went inside, closing the door behind him. He was tired and going over to his bed, he undressed, putting his clothes on the chair. He then raised the mosquito net of his cot and got in. Strickland lay under the muslin veil and listened. The forest was quiet. Only the cicadas stirred occasionally in the stillness. Their rhythmic music was like a narcotic and soon the pilot was asleep.

FIVE

When Strickland woke the next morning the sun was already high in the sky, the shutters of his room lit by its rays. Beyond the hut the cicadas chirped madly and monkeys chattered in the trees. The pilot lay on his bunk and wondered where he was. He had been dreaming he was in France again, but he could see that he was alone and he did not recognise his quarters. His gaze wandered to the shelf on the opposite wall and he saw the photograph of Ensign Aoki and he remembered. He was on the island. The Englishman yawned and levering himself out of bed, he stretched his long limbs. In spite of the strange surroundings and the shortness of the bed, he had slept well. He saw there was a pitcher and a bowl on the table by the window and he padded over to it.

The pilot filled the bowl with water and began to wash his face, the coldness reviving him and dissolving the bonds of sleep which enveloped his body. There was a small mirror above the basin and Strickland peered into it, seeing his reflection for the first time in almost a week. He was shocked at what he saw. The face that stared out at him was in stark contrast to the one he knew. His nose was broken and his blue eyes were sunken. Under the left eye was a dark bruise the size of a plum. The clean shaven jawline had gone and was replaced by a scraggy blond stubble. His face was sallow and gaunt and he had lost weight. Strickland rubbed his grizzled chin. The rough beard and his sunken eyes aged him and gave him an ascetic appearance, like an Old Testament prophet or a desert father.

He looked away from the mirror and picking up a towel, he dried his face. The pilot replaced it and walked over to the chair and put on his clothes. His uniform, or what remained of it, was grimy and stained with salt, but it was still a uniform. Despite his dishevelled appearance, the tropical flying kit and the RAF insignia above his breast pocket were a vivid reminder to Strickland of his identity. He put his shirt over his head, then put on his shorts and fastened them, noticing that he needed one less hole in the canvas belt. He found a pair of straw sandals by the bed and placed his feet in them. They were too short and his toes stuck out over the end, but they would do. He checked his appearance in the mirror, ran his fingers through his hair and turned away. The pilot went over to the mesh door, opened it and stepped onto the sunny porch.

The cicadas sang shrilly in the heat and the compound was white in the sun. Strickland surveyed his surroundings and looking up, he saw the mountain rise above the green mantle of forest. He remembered how, only a few days ago, he had flown over it as he made a final turn and prepared to head for home. If he had not seen the wake of the submarine, he would have continued on and doubtless he would have arrived safely back at base. Instead fate ensured that he discovered the submarine, attacked it and was shot down. All this he knew. Yet he wondered what had happened in his absence? Back at base the officer in the control tower would have spent the rest of the day vainly searching the skies for his plane and when the sun went down that evening and he had still failed to return and having no other information as to his whearabouts, the wing commander would have posted him as 'missing'. A notice would be pinned to the operations board outside the mess hall, informing the men of the news and they would shrug their shoulders and shake their heads, as yet another comrade was claimed by the war. The CO would wait for any further news and if there was still none after a week, he would write a letter to his parents informing them that their son had failed to return from patrol and that he should be considered to have been killed. Perhaps his CO had already written the letter. The pilot prayed that he had not and that when he did, it would somehow fail to reach his parents. The thought of his mother opening that small brown envelope was almost more than he could bear. He wished he could reassure her that he was still alive.

Strickland stood there gazing up at the mountain, which shimmered above the forest in the heat and did not know whether to curse or bless the island. He looked away and closing the door behind him, he walked over to Hayama's quarters, his sandals scraping across the dusty compound. He ascended the steps of the captain's hut and seeing that the door was open, he pushed open the fly screen and went inside. Hayama was sitting at his desk annotating his collection of butterflies in a large leatherbound ledger, a pen in his hand. He looked up and saw a tall figure framed against the light of the doorway and put down his pen.

'Good morning,' he said. 'Did you sleep well?'

'Yes, thanks. That was a fine supper last night.'

'Well, you must congratulate Ito for that. He is an excellent cook. Breakfast?'

'That would be nice.'

'Come and sit down,' and Hayama called out over his shoulder, telling his cook to bring some tea and to prepare breakfast for his guest.

Strickland took off his sandals and sat down on the tatami and the captain got up from his desk to join him. He was not in uniform, and instead wore his white kimono. Embroidered across the front panels were red silk peonies. The heraldic flower was divided into four petals and surrounded with a hexagonal border. Sitting there smiling and cross-legged on the tatami, Hayama looked like a Meiji lord content in his surroundings. With his collection of butterflies arranged on one wall, the painted silk screen behind him and the pair of swords on the rack above his bed, you could imagine the captain was sitting at home in Nagasaki, rather than on a remote tropical island thousands of miles away.

'Forgive me for not being in uniform. It's Sunday today and everyone here rests.'

The sense of time had completely deserted the pilot since he had been on the island and the idea that actual days, let alone weeks and months, existed had become alien to him. It had been the case ever since his watch was smashed during one of his interrogation sessions.

'I had no idea what day it was.'

'I insist the men take a day off on Sunday. They don't have leave and cannot get away from the island, but at least they can relax. They usually have games on the beach, or else they just rest and play cards in their quarters. What would you like to do?'

'I thought I might explore. I need the exercise.'

'Of course. I quite understand. There's a trail that leads up to the mountain. It's hard work, but when you get to the top there is a wonderful view. You can see for miles. We have an observation platform there. Don't worry I shan't expect a report.'

The pilot smiled at his companion.

'A trip up the mountain sounds good.'

A noise came from the kitchen and Ito emerged from behind the screen with a tray of breakfast, together with a pot of tea and two cups. He laid the tray on the table and set a bowl of chopped mangoes and a glass of goat's milk before the pilot. He then placed the teapot and cups in the middle and taking the tray, he departed without a word. Strickland drank the glass of milk and putting it down, he picked up a pair of chopsticks and began to eat the mango. The fruit was ripe and juicy and tasted as if it had just fallen from the tree.

Hayama had already had his breakfast and as his guest ate the mango, he took the pot and filled their cups. The pilot soon finished the fruit and together the officers sat there sipping their tea. The room was quiet, the only sound being the cicadas' singing and the occasional rustle of the palm trees in the breeze. Strickland noticed the pair of swords above the captain's bed.

Both were encased in brown leather scabbards, although one was larger and the other more like a dirk.

'Are they yours?' asked the pilot, looking at the weapons. Hayama turned and followed his gaze to the rack above his bed.

'Yes. They're from Kyoto where all the best swords are made. They're very old and have been in my family for many generations. Here, let me show you,' and getting up the captain went over to his bed and took the swords from the rack. He returned and sat down and removed the weapons from their scabbards, laying them both out on the table. The pilot could see that despite their undoubted age, the swords were well kept, the hilts carefully polished.

'They're in wonderful condition.'

'The climate is not good, but I try and keep them as best as I can. They're sacred.'

'Like family relics?'

It was an apt description and the captain nodded.

'Yes. All samurai families have at least one sword in their possession. Sometimes they have several and they are always kept in the family shrine. We pay homage to them just as we honour our ancestors, because the sword is the soul of the samurai. The two cannot be separated.'

'I see,' said the Englishman.

'This shorter one is the *tanto*,' and Hayama drew it and presented it to Strickland. 'It's more a dagger really and is kept in the warrior's belt. Sometimes it is used together with the sword. But you must be a skilled samurai to do so.'

The pilot admired the blade and the embossed gold motif on the hilt.

'The other one is the *katana*,' and the captain drew it and offered the weapon to his guest. The pilot put down the *tanto* and took up the longer sword. The *katana* was heavier and yet it was perfectly balanced. He ran his eye along the elegant curve of the blade, towards the sharp point at the end.

'This type of sword has no peer. If it were ever used against another weapon, it would break it in half.'

Strickland turned it over and inspected the inlaid hilt.

'The *katana* has an illustrious history. The first Mongol invasion of Japan by Kublai Khan was driven back by warriors using their swords. The Mongols had never seen anything like it. The *katana* could cut down a horse and rider with one blow. Can you imagine? Such was the fury of the samurai's attack, the enemy were routed and retreated to their ships. Later that night a storm blew up, damaging many of the vessels at anchor.'

'Did the Mongols return?'

Hayama shook his head.

'They were in no state to face the samurai again and they sailed back to Korea, taking a whole month to complete the journey. They had lost 13,000 men, which was one third of their total, including a high-ranking Korean general. But the Khan had never been thwarted and vowed revenge, this time to take all of Japan. He was patient and for seven long years he prepared his invasion force. Six hundred warships were ordered from southern China, in addition to a further 900 from Korea. The force consisted of 140,000 men, divided into two armies which set sail, intending to land at Hakata Bay in the north. But the samurai were waiting for them and under cover of darkness they rowed out to the enemy fleet in small boats, boarded the vessels and cut the invaders to pieces.

'On one occasion thirty samurai swam out to a ship, decapitated the entire crew and then swam back. One samurai named Jiro Kusano led a raid in broad daylight and set fire to a ship, even though his left arm had been completely severed. The battles raged for days until a further Mongol force arrived and anchored off the island of Takashima. The samurai launched wave after wave of attack against this new force, but were beaten back by the sheer number of the invaders. By now they were exhausted and outnumbered and had lost many men, and it was plain the Khan's forces would now be able to land. So the people prayed and made offerings to the gods who heard them and sent a divine wind, the *kamikaze*, which destroyed the ships. The entire Mongol fleet was obliterated by a typhoon.'

'What happened to the great Khan?'

'I presume he went back to his harem in Xanadu,' replied Hayama with a smile.

Strickland cradled the weapon in his hands. The same weapon that had so nearly beheaded him. Even holding the sword made him feel like a samurai.

'How do they manage to make the blade so strong?' he asked, handing the *katana* back to its owner.

The captain took it, running his fingers down the steel.

'Each swordsmith has his own particular method whose secret is jealously guarded and handed down from father to son by word of mouth.'

'Do they still make them in the traditional way?'

'Yes, but there are only two or three men left in Japan now who could make such a sword. In times gone by there would have been many such men. A good swordsmith was as valuable to the *daimyo* as the samurai they armed.'

Hayama turned the sword over so that its blade gleamed coldly, like moonlight on a wave.

'The sword itself is welded from two pices of metal, one of wrought iron and another of tool steel. The iron gives it strength, the steel gives it its edge. The swordsmith would first heat a lump of crude iron and flatten it into a number of thin plates, which were then forged together into a heavier piece of steel called *uagane*. This was welded together many times with the soft iron core called *shingane*.'

'That's a lot of work for a single weapon.'

'Yes, but this was only the beginning of an even longer process, which gave the swordsmith two grades of steel to work with. He used the laminated steel for the core, and the tool steel for the exterior. The sword was then subjected to a series of heating and quenching processes to produce the cutting blade.

Finally, it was polished with ever finer grades of abrasive stone, which produces this pattern,' and Hayama tilted the sword in the light, so that Strickland could see the wavy lines running down the blade. 'This effect is called *yakiba* and only the finest swords have it.'

The pilot pointed to the other weapon on the table.

'What about this one?'

'The *tanto*?' asked the captain, putting down the longer weapon and picking up the other. 'This is made using the same method, but it is not as strong. Even so it's very handy and easier to conceal.'

Hayama put the dagger down and refilled both their cups from the pot and the officers sat there drinking their tea, the swords lying on the table between them. The paradox was not lost on either man.

Their countries were at war and their traditions could not have been more different. But what had begun as enmity had been transformed if not quite into friendship, then at least into an understanding. Strickland remembered how little animosity his father held for the Germans, even though he had spent four years fighting them in the trenches of Flanders. It was as if the world had to go through such convulsions in order for humanity to rediscover civilisation. Attila the Hun had reached the gates of Rome and Europe was laid waste by the Barbarian tribes, putting an entire civilisation to the torch. The Palmyrans celebrated their sacking of Egypt by immolating the libraries at Alexandria, which burned for three days and nights. Centuries of scholarship and learning reduced to ash and scattered by the four winds. War, it seemed, was a fire which raged unchecked until there was nothing left to burn and it finally extinguished itself.

The pilot's gaze fell upon the gold emblem on the swords' hilts.

'Is this a particular type of flower?'

'It's a peony. Our family crest,' and the captain pointed to the design on his kimono.

'What's the significance?'

'Well, it's a sad tale and possibly apocryphal, but we abide by it nonetheless. One of my ancestors, Keizo Hayama, was slain by a rival samurai called Ko Goto. Legend has it that Goto was furious with my ancestor for taking his favourite geisha, who was very beautiful. In fact my ancestor had merely offered the woman protection, because her master was crazed with jealousy and would beat her if she so much as looked at another man. Anyway, Goto demanded that his honour be restored and he challenged Keizo to single combat. Whoever won the contest would have the geisha. It was a foolish thing to do because my ancestor was an excellent swordsman, but Goto would not back down and my ancestor was obliged as a samurai to accept the challenge. Sure enough when the day of the fight came the man was soundly beaten and my ancestor was within his rights to kill him, but he refused. He had not issued the challenge and he had no particular argument with the idiot Goto. Unfortunately, that was his mistake because what the other samurai lacked in courage and chivalry, he more than made up for in deviousness and cowardice.

'Some time later Goto pretended that he wanted to make it up with my ancestor, to let bygones be bygones and asked him to come to his house for supper. He told Keizo to bring the geisha too, just to show that he had no hard feelings. Well, my ancestor didn't want to go, but he couldn't really refuse a fellow samurai's offer of hospitality, especially after what had just happened. Then, the night before my ancestor was due to visit his adversary, the geisha had a dream. She dreamt that Keizo went to Goto's house and was offered a bouquet of peonies and as he accepted them, he was ambushed by his enemy's henchmen who charged at him with their swords. Mortally wounded he managed to escape, but only out into the roadside where he lay beneath a tree. Weeping, the geisha tended to him as he bled to death. The next morning she told Keizo about this dream. My ancestor listened patiently and did not dismiss it as the ramblings of a hysterical woman.

He was a poet and often his poetry came to him in dreams. He told the woman that she did not have to go, but that he must fulfill his duty. And so he put on his best suit and set off on a cold winter's day. The geisha, however, ignored his order to stay behind and instead followed him through the snow. When Keizo got to Goto's house he was alone and the samurai asked him where the geisha was and my ancestor told him that she had a chill and couldn't come.

'Goto looked disappointed, but only because he wanted to slaughter them both. Instead he would have to make do with my ancestor and so he laughed and told Keizo that he had a special gift for him: a beautiful bouquet of flowers even though it was the middle of winter. And, just as the woman had predicted in her dream, Keizo was offered a bunch of peonies by one of Goto's family. As he held them to his face, Goto's thugs leapt from behind a screen and attacked my ancestor, running their swords through him time and time again. Nevertheless, Keizo managed to beat them off and staggered out into the road, where he lay down beneath an oak tree. The geisha had been waiting outside and seeing him collapse, she ran to his side and tried to staunch his wounds. Sadly, it was to no avail and he bled to death. The geisha hurried home to tell the family what had happened. But when they arrived there was no sign of Keizo's body, just a patch of bright red peonies in the snow. So they built a shrine in his memory and that is why the flower is our emblem.'

'What happened to the geisha?'

'She tied a stone around her neck, threw herself into a river and drowned.'

'And what about Goto?'

'I'm sure he became a *daimyo*.'

Strickland looked at the sword in Hayama's hands. He understood why the captain revered it so much.

'You said your ancestor was a poet. Can you recite any of his poetry?'

'Of course. He wrote many verses,' and Hayama began to sing.

Your voice is like the wind in the trees
That whispers to me
As I walk alone in the forest.
My journey is long and arduous
But your voice is heavenly music…

The captain finished his song and laid the *katana* down on the table. The sun glanced in through the open window, making the swords' blades gleam. Strickland looked at the weapons that lay before him: these objects of terrible beauty and destruction.

'You must be proud of your ancestor.'

'I am. I honour all my ancestors, but Keizo is the most illustrious. Since his death these swords have been handed down from father to son. My father gave them to me before I left for the Pacific. I must be a great disappointment to him,' and Hayama gazed sadly at the weapons on the table.

'Why do you say that?'

The captain raised his eyes and the look he gave Strickland was one of profound unhappiness.

'I come from a family of samurai, but I have never killed an enemy. Where is the honour in that?'

Strickland said nothing and for the first time he felt sympathy for the captain. Here was a man bound by an ancient martial code who, instead of fighting as a warrior as his ancestors had done, had been sent to a remote island in the South Pacific. A silence came between them like the calm before a storm when the birds stop singing, the sky darkens and the wind drops. Eventually the pilot spoke.

'Am I the enemy?'

'You were the enemy. But I did not kill you.'

'Why?'

Hayama let out a long sigh, the sort a man makes when he sees there is a hole in the bottom of his boat and knows that he is a long way from the shore.

'I don't know. And I don't think that I will ever know.'

Strickland sat there in silence. He wanted to help the captain in some way, say something that would remove his burden of guilt.

'Hayama, I must thank you for saving my life.'

'There's no point in thanking me. You must thank the gods. It was they who saved you.'

'Then I thank them.'

'Good. Honour them. They have their reasons.'

The captain managed a smile, but the sadness in his eyes remained.

'It's a beautiful day. You should take your walk.'

The pilot understood and saw that it was time to leave Hayama alone with his swords.

Strickland thanked the captain and getting up, he went to the door. He opened the fly screen and closing it behind him, he walked out across the baking compound. The sun beat down upon him and after a few yards, he could feel the sweat running down the back of his neck. The Englishman wiped a hand through his hair, wishing he had a hat and carried on. Ahead the coconut palms grew thickly like a palisade. In the middle was a trail, which led through the forest. Leaving the camp Strickland headed up the track, the shadows of the trees shading the path before him.

The pilot's presence disturbed a troop of monkeys, which screeched and swooped above his head and he watched as they made graceful arcs through the canopy, swinging from tree to tree. He wondered how the monkeys had come to the island. Had they been brought by earlier visitors as pets and escaped from the ships, or had they come from elsewhere, dislodged by a storm and thrown into the sea where, grabbing a piece of flotsam, they had washed up on the shore? The pilot was sure Hayama would know.

The monkeys disappeared into the forest and the path got steadily steeper as Strickland made his way up the mountain. He noticed a variety of different trees interspersed among the palms, many of them bearing fruit. There were paw-paw and mango, carob and caraway as well as clumps of plantains. Among the boughs were lichens and orchids and plants with great flowers, which oozed nectar and attracted scores of butterflies, as well as the occasional hummingbird. It seemed the island was a tropical larder, a horn of plenty for any animal or Robinson Crusoe who washed up on its shores. There were even goats. Ito tended a pair in the yard and milked them for their breakfast.

Strickland came to a glade and sat down on a smooth boulder to rest. He looked about and marvelled at the forest around him, the trees towering above his head. He could hear water cascading in the distance and assumed it was the stream, which the captain had told him about. He was thirsty and needed a drink and he stood up and followed the sound of rushing water. As the noise grew louder the ground descended sharply and the pilot was careful as he picked his way over the tangle of roots at his feet. Stepping out from behind a great banyan, Strickland saw the bright water tumbling over the rocks as it made its way towards the sea, sunlight flashing on its surface. He went over and bending down, he put his hand into the stream and raised it to his mouth. The water was cold and clear and tasted of flint.

As the pilot drank, he heard another shriller noise above the rushing water. He stopped and listened. There was nothing at first, just the burbling of the stream. Then it came again, a small whimpering like a child's. Strickland stood up and made his way towards the noise. As the whimpering increased, so did the pilot's curiosity. Surely there were no children on the island? The cries came from beneath a low plant, its broad leaves obscuring whatever it was that lay beneath. The pilot bent down and cautiously raised one of the leaves, revealing something small, brown and hairy beneath. He reached out a hand and touched the creature, which was curled up in a ball. It did not flinch, but simply whimpered some more and putting out his hands, Strickland picked it up.

It was not a child, but a monkey. The little macaque must have fallen from its mother's back as she swung through the trees. The pilot raised his eyes to the canopy above him, and could not see any other monkeys, just the fronds fanning a hot blue sky. The baby macaque shivered in his arms and made small plaintive noises. It looked cold and probably needed feeding. Strickland opened his tunic and put the monkey inside, feeling its soft fur against his bare skin. With the macaque tucked safely inside his shirt, he set off up the path towards the mountain top.

The path got steeper as the pilot climbed and the vegetation thinner and sometimes he had to use his hands to haul himself up the rocky slope. He was careful not to let his new companion fall out, but the monkey seemed quite content and had stopped crying. Soon the forest fell away, the coconut palms and banyans replaced by clumps of bamboo and elephant grass. As Strickland walked through the grass he disturbed myriads of white butterflies, which rose in a pale cloud and flitted about his head before settling again. Eventually the grass gave way to bare rock, until there was only the escarpment left to climb. One half was sheer and fell away to the sea, which dashed itself against the rocks hundreds of feet below. It was impossible to traverse and so the pilot walked round to the other side, hearing the sound of falling water as he approached. Turning a corner he saw the cascade tumbling from the bare rock and beneath it the pool Hayama had told him about. The stream poured out from a fissure in the cliff and Strickland assumed there must be a subterranean spring. It was clear and bright and the water looked invitingly cool. The pilot's thirst had returned after his steep climb and he bent down and dipped his hand into the pool and drank. It tasted less flinty than further down the hill, although it was just as cold.

Strickland wiped his mouth and stood up. With one hand holding the macaque inside his shirt, he jumped across the stream and walked around the escarpment. Standing before him beneath a roof of palm fronds was the observation platform. It was well hidden and would have been almost impossible to spot from the air. He could only have been a couple of hundred feet away when he had flown past it and yet he had seen nothing. He wondered what the Japanese observer had thought with his Spitfire coming so close. A soldier stood smoking a cigarette, which he put out when he saw the pilot approach. The private bowed and the Englishman nodded and said 'good morning' and the Japanese smiled and returned the greeting in his own language.

The pilot stepped onto the platform and looked out across the ocean. All around the sea's skin stretched away before him, its scales glittering beneath the sun. Here and there bright green patches ringed with white indicated other islands and atolls. In the distance a solitary ship steamed, its wake cutting a pale swath through the dark blue water. The ship was most likely American or at least an ally, but it was too far away to distinguish clearly without binoculars. The destroyer was doubtless hunting for the last remaining Japanese submarines in the area. Beyond the ship the silver sea crawled towards the horizon, the sky a wall of blue behind.

The monkey woke up and started to cry and Strickland decided to return to the camp. He left the soldier to his solitary duty and jumping across the stream, he made his way back along the escarpment.

He slid swiftly down the volcanic clinker, a fine grey dust rising up into the air as he went. The rocky path levelled out and soon he had left the clumps of elephant grass with their clouds of butterflies and entered the cool shade of the forest. The journey down the hill was much easier and the pilot did not need to stop and drink from the stream as he passed the giant banyan where he had found the little macaque. With one hand cradling the monkey he wandered down the trail, the sunlight glancing through the trees, leaving bright pools across the path.

A few minutes later Strickland emerged from the forest and walked out across the burning compound. He carried on past the soldiers' quarters and the mess hall and went up to Hayama's cabin.

He ascended the steps and could see him working at his desk. The pilot tapped on the frame and pushing the fly screen open, he stepped inside. The captain stopped writing and looked up.

'Enjoy your walk?'

'Yes, thank you. You can see for miles.'

'I know. I sometimes go there myself. It's good to get away from the camp occasionally. Have you been collecting coconuts?' said Hayama and he pointed to the bulge in the pilot's shirt.

'Not exactly,' and putting a hand inside, Strickland produced the monkey.

'*Oya maa!* Where did you get that?'

'I found it under a bush. It must have fallen off its mother's back,' and the pilot offered the captain the macaque.

Hayama took the monkey and held it, tickling it with his finger as if it were a small child. It had large sympathetic brown eyes and naked fleshy ears, which jutted out like a clown's. The monkey whimpered softly and the captain turned it over in his hands, looking for any signs of injury. Fortunately there were none, the macaque having had a soft landing when it fell. He gazed down at the fine white hair on its stomach and saw the genitalia between its legs.

'It's a boy,' he announced, like a proud parent. 'What shall we call him?'

Strickland smiled. He thought Hayama the naturalist would take an interest, but he did not think he would go so far as to adopt the creature.

'Well, if Hitler is the organ grinder, who's his monkey?'

'Mussolini?'

The pilot looked at the brown furry ball in the captain's hands.

'That's a little unfair.'

'What, to that idiot?'

'No, to monkeys. I was thinking rather of Neville Chamberlain.'

'Wonderful! Chamberlain it is!' the captain exclaimed and he bent down and kissed the monkey's soft fur. 'Do you think he's hungry?'

'Probably. What are we going to feed him?'

'Let's try a bit of fruit to see if he's been weaned. I'll give him some mango. It's very digestible.' Hayama handed the monkey back to the pilot and went off to the kitchen.

Strickland held the warm bundle, which seemed quite content and soon the captain returned with a small bowl of diced yellow fruit. He dipped his fingers into the mango and picked up a piece and held it in front of the monkey's nose. The macaque sniffed the morsel, then took it with its tiny paw and ate. Hayama repeated the action and the monkey did the same, slowly chewing the mango, its brown simian eyes fixed trustingly upon the captain. Soon the bowl was empty and the Japanese officer put it down and taking the macaque from Strickland, he spoke soothingly.

'There we go. How was that? Did you like the mango? Delicious, isn't it? Now you must rest. Where would you like to sleep?'

The pilot watched all this with a smile on his face. Hayama seemed transformed, his earlier despondency having apparently vanished. Now that he had something to care for, his melancholy and lassitude had been replaced by a cheerful ebullience. The captain searched for a suitable place and saw a box by his bed, where he kept his charts. Holding the macaque with one hand, he tipped the charts out onto the bed and picking up his pillow, he put it in the bottom of the container. He then placed the monkey on the pillow and put the box back in the corner. He watched over it for a while and satisfied, he picked up the charts and turned to the pilot.

'I think he'll be fine. He's been weaned, which is a relief. We'll let him sleep.'

'He liked the mango.'

'They do. They're not fussy, they like anything really. Roots, leaves, nuts, fruit. Just like us,' and the captain grinned. 'How about some lunch? Ito's prepared a picnic. I thought we'd go down to the beach and eat it there.'

'OK,' said the pilot. Not only was he hungry after his long

walk, but he also felt hot and clammy and wanted a bathe.

The captain put the charts down on his desk and went into the kitchen, returning with two small parcels in his hand and a canteen. Hayama and Strickland left the macaque in its box and together they made their way down to the beach. As they approached the shore, the pilot could hear cries and laughter echoing through the trees and as the palms gave way to the sand, he saw the soldiers playing volleyball. The men did not notice the officers at first and carried on with their game, until one of them shouted out and the entire troop stopped and standing to attention they all bowed as one, the ball bouncing away across the sand and into the sea.

'*Tsuzukeru shinshi*,' said Hayama.

'*Heitai-san!*' replied the men and one of them ran off to retrieve the ball bobbing in the surf.

The soldier dashed into the water and picking up the ball, he ran back to his comrades and they started their game again. Hayama and Strickland sat down beneath a palm tree to watch, their bento boxes on their laps. The pilot opened his and found some dried fish, a ball of rice with green pepper, some bean curd and a small pot containing soy sauce. Using his fingers he dipped the fish in the bean curd and put it into his mouth, finding the saltiness of the dried fish leavened by the sweetness of the curd. He took the lid off the pot and picking up a lump of rice, he dabbed it in the sauce and ate. The captain also began his own picnic and together the two of them ate their lunch and watched as the men threw the ball about, leaping at the net to smash it over the side, or else trying to prevent it from coming into their own half. Sometimes the strike would beat the opposition and a new game commenced; a man would dive across the sand and punch the ball to a teammate, who would flick it on to cheers from his own side and shouts from the other.

'They're good,' said Strickland.

'I know. I taught them myself,' replied the captain, proud of his men's ability. 'I learned to play in Hawaii.'

'It wasn't all spying then?'

Hayama laughed and wiped his mouth with a napkin.

'Some of my best work was done at the beach!'

The pilot looked out towards the reef and saw the breakers crashing white against the coral barrier.

'Did you ride the waves on those long wooden boards?'

'You mean did I surf?' asked the captain and the pilot nodded. 'I did try, but it takes a lot of practice. To be any good you really have to start from the day you can swim.'

'You liked Hawaii then?'

'Yes I did. They're an island race too.' Hayama smiled. 'They have an interesting history. Like the Carolines, they began as volcanic eruptions in the sea and life evolved in its own unique way. It really was a paradise. There were no mosquitoes, reptiles, or rats. Almost everything unpleasant in the islands was brought by man. The first settlers were the Polynesians, the greatest seafaring people on earth.'

Strickland picked up a piece of fish and popped the morsel in his mouth and swallowed.

'With the possible exception of the Vikings,' he said.

'Ah! The Norsemen. How could I forget? That's why your country became such a great naval power. All that Viking blood!'

'There are many Norse names where I come from. A chronicler of those times called Bede lived in a monastery by the sea. From the window of his cell he looked out onto the ocean. Over the horizon lay Denmark and the Vikings. The English never knew when they would come, but when they saw the ships' sails appear on the horizon, everyone fled to the nearest castle. Those who didn't perished. Eventually, the Vikings stopped raiding and stayed and mixed with the local population.'

The captain looked at the pilot and grinned.

'Of course they did. Look at you. Tall, blue-eyed, fair and with that beard!'

The pilot stroked his jaw. The beard no longer itched and he thought he might keep it.

They continued eating their lunch, watching the soldiers play and Strickland thought how similar these men were to his own comrades, as they whiled away their afternoons on the cricket field. Everyone happy under heaven. He finished his food and lay back under the palm trees, watching the rustling fronds swaying in the ocean breeze.

'You must have had mixed feelings about leaving Hawaii.'

'Yes I did. I'd like to go back there. Who knows, maybe after the war?'

The pilot turned onto his side and faced the captain.

'What will you do when the war's over?'

'I haven't really given it much thought. I'd like to do a doctor-ate in entomology. Perhaps in Honolulu. What about you?'

'Finish my degree at Oxford.'

'What were you studying?'

'Greats.'

Hayama looked quizically at his companion.

'What's that?'

'The classics: Latin and Greek.'

'And then?'

'I don't know. Perhaps teaching.'

'You would be a good teacher.'

Strickland was silent and looking away, he watched the waves as they gently lapped the shore. Before the war he had consid-ered joining the church, his faith had always been strong and he admired the monks who had taught him, giving him a sense of man's true place in the world through their own spirituality. The Benedictine philosophy was one of *conversatio morum,* a con-version of manners or more accurately, life. Their teaching left a watermark on the child's soul, which was visible only when held up to the light, but remained indelible to the end. Yet as the war continued the Englishman's belief in God had diminished. It was not so much the personal loss of his friends and comrades, that he knew was fate. Sometimes the pilot questioned the exist-ence of a deity that allowed such carnage to rage unabated. Was this not a time for divine intervention? An act of God? Then he remembered something a priest had once told him at school.

'In the evening of life we shall be examined in love.'

'Who said that?'

'A Spanish friar called John of the Cross. He was a doctor of the Christian church.'

The captain picked up a shell and dug at the sand.

'Tell me about this John of the Cross.'

The pilot gazed out across the lagoon as he recalled his studies of the saint.

'He was a sixteenth-century Spanish mystic who led a humble life at a time when the Catholic church was not especially known for its humility. He was so devout that his own order imprisoned him because his holiness embarrassed them. He wrote several works about faith and how to lead a life devoted to Christ. He also wrote a considerable amount of poetry.'

'Can you remember any?'

'It was a long time ago,' said the pilot. 'But I remember one in particular,' and he began to recite a poem that he had learned as a boy.

My love is as the hills,
The lonely valleys clad with forest trees,
The rushing, sounding rills,
Strange isles in distant seas,
Lover-like whisperings, murmurs of the breeze.

My love is hush-of-night,
Is dawn's first breathings in the heaven above,
Still music veil'd from sight
Calm that can echoes move,
The feast that brings new strength – the feast of love!

Strickland finished and a silence lay between them. The soldiers had gone and there was just the whisper of palm fronds and the waves lapping the shell-strewn shore. Hayama looked out towards the distant surf and the horizon beyond and was filled with a sense of peace. He had not known anything like it since the war began. This man had come into his life like some winged messenger from the gods. Why had they sent him? The captain was sure there had to be a reason. He turned towards the pilot.

'Will you write it down for me?' he asked.

'Of course,' came the reply.

Strickland sat up and in the distance he could see a lithe, young figure bounding over the rocks. The man jumped down onto the sand and came running towards them.

Moments later a breathless Ito slumped down at their feet. He was wearing a pair of swimming trunks, his dark hair matted, his body wet and glistening. In his hand he held a harpoon. Around his back was a string bag and unfastening it, he put a hand inside and produced his spoils. He held out a dead octopus, lank and leathery like a punctured football.

'*Tako!*' he said, showing the tentacled creature to his captain.

'Well done, we'll eat it for supper. Where did you catch it?'

'*Ni nanpa taiisan,*' replied the orderly, still breathless from his exertions.

'What did he say?' asked Strickland.

'He said he caught it out by the wreck. There's an old Dutch merchant ship, which lies in a few fathoms of water near the reef. It was probably damaged by a typhoon, then sank as it made its way into the harbour. Ito does most of his fishing there.'

'I'd like to see it,' said the pilot.

'Ito, why don't you show Mr Strickland the wreck? Perhaps you might catch another octopus, this one is rather small.'

'*Heitai-san,*' answered the orderly.

'And you can practice your English too.'

'Yes ... sir,' replied Ito with a bashful look.

'I'll take this home and put it in some water.' Hayama got up and picking up the octopus and the empty bento boxes, he walked back towards the camp.

The other two watched him go. As he disappeared into the trees, Strickland turned to his companion.

'Will you show me the wreck?'

'Of course … come on,' said the orderly and he got up.

Ito hopped barefoot across the burning sand and the Englishman followed. They walked round to the edge of the harbour and climbed the great boulders along the promontory. Once on top of the spur, Ito leapt from rock to rock with sure-footed grace and Strickland jumped after him as best he could. When he reached the end the orderly stopped and waited for the pilot to catch up. Strickland arrived a little out of breath and looking back, he could see the pale beach curving like a blade towards the jetty on the far side. Before him the sea echoed and boomed. He watched as the waves pounded the coral, the surf exploding in a white cannonade across the reef. The wind whipped the tops of the waves so that a fine mist rose from their crests, before they came crashing down upon the coral. The air was thick with salt and the pilot breathed in deeply, filling his lungs.

'The wreck is down there,' said the orderly, pointing at the surface which shimmered a few feet below.

Strickland peered into the water, but could see nothing except the sunlight wobbling on the waves.

'How deep is it?'

'Not much. Maybe twenty feet. I show you,' and Ito picked his way down the rocks to the shore.

The pilot followed and joined him on top of a large, black slab which stuck out above the water.

'There … now you see it,' said his companion pointing into the depths.

The water was as clear as *sake* and the pilot could see schools of brightly coloured fish swimming below. The fish would flit back and forth and suddenly scatter as a predator swam by. There was an abundance of coral of varying shapes and hues, some waving like fans, others static like the branches of petrified trees. And yet, as the pilot gazed at all the marine life below, he could not see any sign of the sunken vessel.

'There's plenty of coral, but where's the ship?'

'It is beneath. The coral grow above wreck.'

Strickland looked again and as his eyes became accustomed to the variegated mass of marine life, he could make out a large shape lying perpendicular to the shore. It was the Dutch merchantman. The seabed was so shallow that when the ship sank its main deck must have been above water. Over the years the tide and storms had levelled the vessel, so that only its hull remained on the bottom. He wondered what had happened to the crew. Had they been rescued? Or were they forced to survive on the island until they finally perished? Perhaps that was how the monkeys had arrived.

'You are ready?' asked Ito, grasping the harpoon in one hand and holding his mask in the other.

'You go first. I'll follow,' the pilot replied and the orderly hopped in, his body barely making a splash. Strickland waited until he emerged and stripping off his clothes and sandals, he dived after him into the sea.

The Englishman swam beneath the waves and then broke the surface, shaking the water from his hair. He saw Ito grinning at him and suddenly they both started laughing. Neither of them knew why they were laughing, perhaps it was just the sheer pleasure of being in the water. The sea echoed to the sound of their happiness, their voices rising above the crashing surf.

'Go on, show me the wreck,' said Strickland, still smiling.

'*Oke*,' replied Ito and putting on his mask, he flipped over and disappeared beneath the surface.

The pilot followed and together they swam down towards the merchantman. Strickland did not have a mask and opening his eyes, he found the underwater world oddly translucent, shapes and colours melding together in an aqueous light. He lost sight of Ito and continued on towards the wreck. Strickland grabbed a piece of coral on the ship's deck and hung onto it, marvelling at the seascape around him. He felt he had been transported to another world, a silent numinous kingdom full of strange delights. A variety of fish surrounded him, quite unafraid of this interloper and stretching out a hand they nibbled curiously at his fingers, before dashing away again. He looked down and saw a giant clam gape by his foot, a wave of colour pulsing across the fleshy opening of its mouth. As the oxygen in his blood diminished the pilot felt his chest beginning to constrict and looking up, he could see the waves rippling above him like a patch of sky. He let go of the coral branch and kicked, rising in a single glide. His head broke the surface and exhaling he opened his eyes, the sun's glare making him squint. Strickland trod water and soon Ito appeared beside him. In his hand was his harpoon, a blue angel fish twitching on the barbs.

'Take this,' he said, removing the mask from his face and handing it to the pilot. 'You can see wreck much better.'

Strickland took the mask and put it over his head, adjusting it to fit his face. Through the watery pane of glass he saw Ito smiling at him and giving him a thumbs up, he turned and dived again. This time the seabed appeared in sharp relief, the colours no longer unfocused, but varied and bright. Beneath him lay the wreck with its verdant foliage of coral and he swam down towards it, a school of tiny silver fish scattering in his path like bullets. With his hand upon the coral the pilot pulled himself along the wreck, until he came to the shattered mizzen mast encased in a mass of green and red fans waving idly in the current. Before the mast lay the open hatch of the main deck, an ominous black square where fish came and went. The Englishman swam over the opening and felt a chill across his body. He continued on to the bow and with the air in his lungs beginning to fail, he took a final look along the wreck before pushing off and swimming towards the surface.

Strickland emerged with a gasp and removed the mask from his face. He took a gulp of air and spat, then looked about and saw that Ito was paddling near the shore and swam towards him.

'Wonderful!' he said, as he approached. 'All those fish!'

'Yes, there are many fish!' agreed the young Japanese.

'Here take this.' Strickland handed the orderly his mask. 'Go and catch your octopus. I'm going to have a rest.'

'*Oke*,' said Ito, slipping the mask over his head. 'I hope I catch one,' and with that he ducked, disappearing like a cormorant beneath the surface.

The pilot turned and headed back towards the promontory. With a few strokes he reached the wave-spattered shore and trod water as he selected a suitable rock and grabbing one, he hauled himself out of the sea, the waves trying to drag him back. With a final effort Strickland rose clear from the water and climbed up the boulders towards his clothes, but he did not put them on and instead lay down, using his shirt as a pillow. He stretched out on the sun-warmed rocks and soaked up the heavens' rays. The pilot closed his eyes, listening to the surf roaring in his ears and in a short while he dozed off.

He had not been asleep long when a splash of water woke him. He looked up and saw Ito standing over him with an octopus squirming in his hand. The orderly turned the mottled mass inside out and bit it. He then put the dead octopus in his bag and sat down next to him.

'We'll eat well tonight,' said the pilot, raising himself on his elbows.

'Yes. Captain Hayama like octopus very much. But he like this even more,' and he made a snapping motion with his fingers and thumbs.

'Crab?'

'Yes. He love crab. But they are difficult to catch. The crab hide deep. They live out by reef,' and the orderly pointed to the foaming line of surf.

Strickland smiled and lay back again and Ito joined him, taking off his bag. The two men lay there on the rock, sunning themselves like lizards as the waves pumelled the shore. The sky above them was blue and empty and a breeze blew in from the ocean bringing a taste of the sea. The air was soporific and soon they fell asleep. As the afternoon wore on, the sun made its slow way across the heavens, the wind dropped and the sky deepened.

After a while Strickland woke again. His head felt light and his limbs heavy from sleeping in the sun and he decided to have another swim before returning to the camp. Ito dozed quietly beside him. The pilot left him to his slumber and padded over to the large rock and standing on its edge, he flexed his knees and dived in. The water was refreshingly cold and the Englishman struck out towards the reef. As he drew closer, the noise became almost deafening. The pilot went as near as he dared and watched in awed fascination as the waves detonated across the coral, before rising again and rolling in a phalanx towards him. Finally, he turned and swam back to the shore and saw Ito sitting up on the rock.

'You are strong swimmer,' said the orderly, as Strickland hauled himself out of the water.

'I grew up by the sea,' the pilot replied, picking his way towards his companion.

'Ah … like me.'

'Captain Hayama told me that you're from Nagasaki.'

'Yes,' said Ito. 'I'm half man, half fish.'

Strickland smiled and observed the young Japanese. Hayama said that he had compassion, but if that were true it was nothing compared to the orderly's. If it had not been for Ito he would have died in the punishment box. Both of them knew what had happened and both of them realised they must never mention it.

'It's getting late,' the pilot said as he looked out to sea at the westward sun and began to put on his clothes. 'We should get back to the camp.'

'I hope the captain-san will be happy with my fish,' replied the orderly, picking up the bag which contained his catch.

'I'm sure he will,' answered his companion and together they made their way over the rocks towards the beach.

When they reached the camp the two of them parted. Ito went

into the yard behind Hayama's quarters and the pilot returned to his own cabin. He was tired from swimming and lying out in the sun and after a quick shower he went inside and lay down on his bed. Strickland closed his eyes, enjoying the respite from the day's heat. He lay there in the gloom, listening to the diminishing sounds of the forest as the sun set beyond the trees.

Later, the pilot went over to the captain's hut and found his friend happily playing with the macaque, who seemed to have taken to his new guardian. Hayama had made a collar and fastened it with a long chain so that Chamberlain could run freely around his quarters without escaping. The radio was tuned to a station playing popular music and the atmosphere was happy. They dined on Ito's grilled octopus and after supper the captain brought out his set of Mahjong and sat down to teach the pilot how to play. He built the walls containing the various characters and described the importance of the dragons, the seasons and the four winds. They played late into the night, constantly refilling each other's glasses with *sake*. There was laughter and music and outside the pale moon shone and cicadas sang in the trees.

SIX

Strickland spent the following days fishing and swimming with Ito out by the wreck and whiled away the evenings with Hayama, where they would talk long into the night. Sometimes he would go for walks alone in the forest and come back with his arms laden with fruit. He would take whatever he had picked around to the yard at the back and would often find the orderly there, either tending the chickens or filleting and salting fish and hanging them out to dry on long bamboo poles. The pilot also made himself a rudimentary fishing rod, which he used with some success. Ito had given him an old reel which he no longer used, preferring the harpoon, and Strickland had gone and cut down a length of bamboo from the forest. After stripping and sanding the wood, the pilot had hammered some nails along the shaft and using a pair of pliers, he bent them over to make the eyes. He then attached the reel to its base with some twine and threaded the line through the metal hoops. It was not perfect and the line occasionally snagged as he cast, but it worked well enough. He used either a lure, which he had cut from a tin can and hammered flat, or a cork and a hook which he baited with fish. Once he caught a wahoo that must have weighed seven or eight pounds.

Early one morning Ito was standing in the sunlit yard, wearing nothing but a loincloth as he salted his catch. He rubbed the flakes firmly into the fillet before hanging it on a bamboo pole, which he placed in the sun. One of the goats cried and turning around he saw the Englishman coming towards him.

'*Ohayo gozaimasu, ogenki desu-ka?*' he said, making the smallest of bows.

'*Ohayo gozaimasu, oke domo arigato,*' answered Strickland, who now spoke a few rudimentary words of Japanese. He bent down and stroked one of the goat's brown ears and the animal bleated contentedly. He patted the beast and stood up.

'Working hard?'

'Yes, today is special day,' said the orderly in a hushed voice, tapping his lips with his forefinger and indicating the commander's quarters behind him.

'Oh, why's that?' whispered the pilot.

'Captain Hayama. His birthday is today. He think we do not remember. But we have big surprise.'

'Really?'

'Yes, in evening we will make performance and sing.'

Strickland smiled at the prospect.

'I'm sure the captain will enjoy it.'

'I hope so. But you must say nothing. The captain-san does not know …'

The pilot nodded. Hayama had not mentioned his impending birthday and he wondered what he could get him for a present.

'I shan't say a word, I promise,' he said and taking up his rod, he left Ito to his salting.

The Englishman walked out of the yard and made his way down to the beach. At the shore he wandered along the water's edge towards the promontory, his footsteps leaving a trail of wet bruises in the sand. Approaching the spur he climbed up the great boulders and holding his rod with one hand, he put the other out for balance and leapt from rock to rock, until he reached the end. He clambered down onto a flat piece of basalt which formed a natural platform, then unhooked the lure and let it swing freely in the breeze. Strickland held the rod over his shoulder and with a flick of his wrist, he cast the weight into the sea. It landed with a splash and he paused briefly before reeling it in, occasionally flexing the rod from side to side to make the lure appear more fishlike. When it was at the water's edge, he raised the strip of metal and repeated the process. The waves broke against the pilot's legs as he cast and he had to steady himself as the rollers came thundering in, the water foaming white about his feet and dissipating into the rock pools behind.

Strickland enjoyed the solitude of fishing, whether he actually caught anything or not was unimportant. It was the sense of peace and isolation that he loved. It took him back to his childhood when he used to fish for pike in the cold, dark lakes near his home. He admired Britain's often maligned fresh-water predator. They were elusive to catch and, if the fisherman could be bothered, were delicious to eat once the bones were removed. Most people never tried and if they found a pike on the end of their line they simply knocked it on the head and threw it into the bushes. But the pilot actively sought out *esox lucius*, rather than the more favoured carp or trout which shared its water. The pleasure for him was not in the killing or even in the eating, but in catching his prey and playing with it before it finally tired and allowed him to reel it in. He would coax the fish into the shallows and watch as it lay exhausted in the peaty water, its mottled body camouflaged amongst the reeds. The problem was getting the lure out of its mouth, without hurting the fish or losing your fingers. After removing the hook Strickland would place the pike back in the water, his hands beneath its belly as he waited for it to recover. Then, with a flick of its tail, the fish would be gone.

There were stories of pike living up to two hundred years or more. The pilot believed them. He had heard one tale where a female pike weighing almost fifty pounds had been caught in a lake in North Yorkshire at the turn of the century. A thin gold band encircled its throat with the date 1706. It had been part of a breeding stock that had somehow managed to evade capture for all those years. The pike was a most remarkable fish, a survivor that deserved better than to be treated as some sort of piscine vermin. The largest one Strickland had ever caught had weighed sixteen pounds. It took him almost an hour to land. He had to kill the fish as the pike had swallowed the lure whole and it was after dark by the time he got home. Even so his guests were impressed by his catch. Later he gutted and cleaned the fish and baked it in a copper kettle with fennel and onion, garnishing it with parsley and new potatoes. He and his companions dined like princes that night, toasting the quenelled pike with glasses of claret.

The sun beat down upon the water, the shifting sea reflecting its shattered light. The pilot found the constant motion of the waves almost hypnotic as they broke across the reef and charged in a pale battalion towards him, finally dashing themselves against the rocks. After a time Strickland clambered up the spur and stood on top of the boulder where he and Ito dived. He could cast the lure further from here, but if he caught anything he would have to scramble down to the water's edge to retrieve it. The pilot tried a few casts above the wreck, hoping to attract the bigger fish, which chased the minnows among the coral. He had no luck and after an hour Strickland decided to stop and reeling in his line, he hooked the lure against the rod and made his way back along the promontory.

The pilot jumped down from the spur and walked along the shell-strewn beach. He needed to get Hayama a birthday present and as he wandered across the sand, he searched for a suitable piece of driftwood. He wanted to carve an icon for the captain who showed a particular interest in John of the Cross, the subject of many of their discussions. It had been a long time since the Englishman had studied the friar and his works and he could only remember a little of his life and teaching and some of his poems, but Hayama was fascinated by the mystic whose asceticism, holiness and quest for spiritual enlightenment resembled the Shinto priests of his own faith.

Strickland continued to look about the beach, picking up the odd piece of jetsam and inspecting it, before discarding it as unsuitable. Then, a few yards away, he saw a piece of timber half-buried in the sand. He put down his fishing rod and pulling out the plank of wood, he saw it would make a perfect panel for his icon. It was the size of a small chopping board and had been bleached by the sun and worn smooth by the tides. With the timber in his hand, the pilot picked up his fishing rod and made his way back through the trees to the camp.

When he arrived at his hut, he left the rod on the porch, pushed open the door and stepped inside, relieved to be out of the sun. Strickland kicked off his sandals and padded over to the desk in the corner and pulling open a drawer, he took out a penknife which had belonged to the hut's previous occupant. The pilot sat down at the desk and began to whittle away at his piece of wood, while Ensign Aoki looked on impassively from his place on the bookshelf. Strickland remained unaware of the man's presence as he continued with his carpentry, scoring at the soft wood with the knife, before blowing away the shavings. He had no idea what Fray Juan actually looked like, only that he had been bearded and small even for his times. His contemporary and spiritual adviser Teresa of Avila had referred to him as her 'little friar'.

Theirs had been a curious relationship. When they first met Teresa was already well known as a doctor of the church and by then middle-aged. The diminutive Juan de Yepes was only twenty-two and had just begun his religious life. But it was a life to which he was well suited. He came from Castile, a land of barren plateaux and endless blue skies, whose silence was echoed only by the wind and the cry of eagles. To the visitor it seemed as if they had come to the edge of the world. This was the country of John of the Cross and, by a happy coincidence, it was also where the Carmelite abbess belonged. When Teresa first met the friar she was impressed not only by his intellect – he had already completed his first degree at the University of Salamanca – but also by his sanctity and immediately accepted him when he asked to join her new 'Discalced' order, finding a house for him and his fellow friars. The Discalceds (literally barefooted) had split from the original Mitigated Rule in order to lead a stricter and more simple life. It was precisely what John had been looking for as he searched for a suitable order in which to practice his faith. He resolutely believed that without constant physical privation, it was impossible to achieve the necessary state of self-abnegation required to attain true holiness. It was only when temporal desire had been properly subsumed into a religious life, that man could truly become a saint. This idea in particular appealed to Hayama.

He told Strickland about Tsunetomo Yamamoto's Hagakure or 'Book of Leaves', the samurai master's own collection of maxims, which the captain used for guidance. There were indeed many similarities between the two writers, despite the obvious differences of their respective cultures. Although one was a soldier and the other a monk, both men desired to attain a state of pure enlightenment and devotion. John through prayer and self-denial and Yamamoto through obedience and self-sacrifice. Hayama said the essence of Yamamoto's teaching lay in the first sentence of his work: '*The way of the samurai is found in death*'.

The pilot saw another parallel with Ignatius of Loyola, the soldier saint who founded the Society of Jesus. As a young man Ignatius had fought against the French at the siege of Pamplona and had been badly wounded. During his long convalescence he read much Christian theology and decided to give up soldiering and devote his life to the church and good works. With the blessing of Rome he established his order whose followers, the Jesuits, eventually spread as far afield as the captain's own country. Ignatius' dramatic conversion of life made perfect sense to Hayama, because the concept of the warrior monk was at the heart of Yamamoto's teachings. The samurai master had written that a monk could not fulfil the Buddhist Way if he did not have compassion on the outside and courage within, and that if a warrior did not have courage on the outside and compassion within, then he could not become a retainer. The monk therefore had to pursue courage with the warrior as his model and the warrior had to pursue the compassion of the monk.

Strickland continued his carving into the afternoon, the knife scoring away at the sea-softened wood. The image of the friar gradually began to appear before him, bearded and with a halo, his right hand raised in a blessing, the forefinger pointing heavenwards. Above the portrait the Englishman had written 'John of the Cross' and below it one of his maxims: *'And where there is no love, put love in and you will draw love out.'*

The pilot blew at the last remaining shavings and wiping away the dust with his fingers, he inspected his work. It was crude and rudimentary and hardly art, but he thought the captain would appreciate the gesture. He put the carving to one side and scooping up the shavings, he put them in the waste-paper basket by his desk. Strickland got up, went over to the door and stood there looking out at the camp. It was late afternoon and the place was quiet except for the cicadas' incessant sobbing among the trees. He turned away and walked over to the bed where he lay down, deciding to rest before the evening's entertainment.

Presently he fell asleep and began to dream. The pilot dreamt that he was out fishing by the wreck when he saw something swimming in the water. At first he thought it was a man, but it swam with too much suppleness and grace to be quite human and he noticed that it had a tail, its scales flashing silver in the sun. Perhaps it was a porpoise. But what was that head? He suddenly realised it was not a porpoise at all, but a merman. He called out to the creature who seemed to hear him, although he would not come any closer. It looked as if the merman was in some sort of distress as he swam this way and that, constantly calling. It was a strange noise, a terrible wailing sound, such as a fish would make if it had vocal chords. Strickland realised the merman was crying. The creature stopped swimming and looked directly at him, his pale eyes filled with tears, his sealion voice half yelp, half croak. The pilot called out, he wanted to help, but the merman came no closer. Then with a final cry, the manfish slipped beneath the waves.

Strickland woke with a shudder and sat up, the merman's face still vivid in his memory. He lay there on the bed looking up at the rafters and wondered what, if anything, his dream meant. He could find no answer. The air at least had cooled and he got up and went over to the basin to wash his face. The water refreshed him and the pilot dried his hands on a towel and glancing in the mirror, quickly combed his hair. Then he put the icon in his pocket and left the hut to see his friend. The captain had just returned from making his daily report at the signals hut and was sitting at his desk with Chamberlain on his lap. He seemed to have a natural affinity with animals; the chickens always came when he called and the goats bleated happily at the sound of his voice. Hayama put his pet down and watched as the monkey scampered off into a corner, picking up a piece of coconut. He turned to the radio behind him, switched it on and began to adjust the dial. He wanted to listen to the Home and Empire service and hear that evening's news. The radio crackled and whined before the voice of the announcer emerged from the ether. The reception was tinny but clear. Satisfied, the captain looked away and saw the pilot standing at the door.

'Good evening,' he said.

'Not disturbing you, am I?' asked Strickland as he entered, removing his sandals and leaving them on the porch.

The captain smiled and shook his head.

'No, no, it's just the news … what's going on at home.'

The pilot felt a sharp pang of guilt. He had hardly thought about 'home' in the last few days, it seemed so far removed from his life on the island.

'Anything happened?'

'Well, the Americans are still bombing Tokyo. They used to bomb only at night, but now they bomb during the day as well. It seems half the city has been razed. So much destruction and for what?'

The question hung in the air like an unanswered prayer, hopeful and hopeless at the same time. The two men said nothing as Chamberlain chittered away in the corner, gnawing on the coconut husk. The captain shrugged his shoulders. There was nothing they could do.

'How about some *sake*?'

'Why not?' answered the pilot.

The Japanese officer called out to his orderly, asking him to bring them some rice wine, the radio's voice playing behind him.

'Take a seat,' he said and Strickland pulled up a chair.

Hayama continued to keep an ear on the report and a look of anguish passed across his face.

'How can you bomb cities?'

The voice behind him carried on, the announcer reading out a litany of destruction across Japan.

'It's madness, I know.'

And Strickland did know. He had seen the damage the Luft-waffe had wrought on London while he had flown sorties above the burning entrails of the city, the sun almost obliterated by dust and smoke. Nor were his own side blameless, Germany had also suffered. In the end it was like for like, a constant war of attrition that led nowhere. For the first time the pilot felt responsible for the destruction, even though he had never dropped a single bomb. He could not pretend that it had nothing to do with him. It was his war too.

The report continued and the officers sat there in silence, listening to a voice that seemed to come from the depths of the underworld. An oracle that spoke of tragedy and sorrow, but which bore no actual relevance to their own lives. All around them the world was being decimated by an extraordinary hurricane, while they remained safe on the island. The eye of this terrible storm.

The pilot shook his head and leant back in his chair.

'When will it ever end?'

'It depends upon America.'

'America?'

The captain nodded, picked up a paper knife and began to turn it in his fingers.

'I am sure America wants to destroy Japan. There can only be one power in the Pacific.'

'Is that possible?'

'To destroy Japan?'

'Yes.'

Hayama shook his head.

'Frankly, no. That is why I am hopeful the Allies and Japan will see sense and make an honourable peace.'

The voice on the radio finally ceased and after a paean to the Emperor, some martial music was played.

'Come on, let's forget about the war and have a drink,' he said, switching off the radio and together they went and sat down on the tatami. As they waited for the orderly to bring them their *sake*, Strickland put a hand inside his pocket and produced the carving.

'I have a present for you,' and he laid his gift on the low table in front of them.

'What's this?' asked the captain, picking up the piece of wood and examining it.

'It's an icon. It's meant to be John of the Cross.'

'Really? The little friar? Thank you. How did you know it was my birthday … ?' and he grinned as he answered his own question: 'Of course, our friend Ito.'

'He only told me this morning.'

'Well, he shouldn't have, but thanks for the thought.' Hayama got up and placed the icon on the shelf above his swords. He stood back and admired it. 'It's beautiful,' he said. 'He looks just how I imagined. He can be my guardian and watch over me.'

The pilot smiled. The present was more successful than he had hoped.

'By the way, how old are you?' he asked.

'Thirty-four,' replied his host as he sat down again at the table. 'Too young for wisdom, too old for youth. How about you?'

'Twenty-five,' said Strickland.

'Really? You look older. I'm sure I do too.'

'It must be the war.'

The captain nodded. It was true. War aged men considerably. If not in their faces, then in their souls. You could see it in their eyes.

There was a clink of china and a smiling Ito appeared with a tray bearing a jug of hot *sake* and three cups. He put it down on the table and on a plate was a cake with a solitary burning candle in the middle.

'Congratulations, captain-san,' said the orderly, bowing.

'Private Ito, you have deliberately disobeyed an order! I should have you flogged!'

The orderly simply smiled. In spite of Hayama's tone of voice, he knew he was joking.

'Most sorry, captain-san.'

Strickland began to sing 'happy birthday' in English and Ito joined him in his own language, as Hayama sat there with an amused look on his face. The pair finished singing and he leant forward and blew out the candle to applause. The captain then picked up a knife and cut some slices from the cake. He offered up the plate and both the pilot and orderly took a piece, with Hayama taking the last. They all began to eat their portion, the officers complimenting Ito on his baking. The sponge was light and buttery and tasted of vanilla and almonds, with a hint of lemon. The captain then poured out the *sake* and Strickland took a cup and raising it, he proposed a toast.

'To friendship,' he said.

'Friendship and long life,' added the orderly and the three of them clinked cups.

'*Kanpai!*' said the captain, before downing his drink.

'*Kanpai!*' repeated his guests.

The trio sat there enjoying their *sake* and birthday cake, when a noise arose from the compound and a chorus of voices could be heard.

'What's this?' asked the captain, hearing the carousing outside. 'What's going on?'

He listened with a bemused look on his face as a troop of

soldiers climbed up the steps of his cabin, singing and playing a variety of musical instruments. There were trumpets and flutes, cymbals and drums, violins and tambourines. They stood there on the verandah singing and playing and making an extraordinary cacophony. The captain leapt to his feet and shouted, trying to look angry. But the more Hayama stamped and swore, the more everyone's mirth increased.

'My birthday is not to be celebrated! I gave strict instructions!' he bellowed.

Even though his voice was harsh, you could see the captain was trying to keep a straight face, his mouth suppressing a smile.

'Damn you insolent sons of bitches! Shut up! Shut up I tell you, you bunch of beardless hermaphrodites! I wouldn't employ you in a brothel!'

The men ignored him and carried on playing their tuneless dirge. Unnoticed, Ito slipped away and the pilot got up and took Hayama by the arm and led him outside. Together the soldiers serenaded the officers across the compound towards the mess, the captain lamely protesting as they walked. When they arrived there was a great cheer from the rest of the company, who were all waiting for them. The tables had been cleared away and replaced by several rows of benches, which faced a curtained stage. Hayama and Strickland were escorted to an empty place in the middle of the front row. They sat down and the band stopped playing and took up some chairs to one side. There was a hush as the house lights dimmed and the babble of voices subsided. The curtain was raised and the audience sat in silent expectation, waiting for the performance to begin.

On stage a woman was sitting at a table combing her hair and singing, her voice accompanied by a violin's mournful note. A light shone through a window revealing a large double bed. As the woman turned and faced the audience, Strickland saw that it was Ito. His face was whitened with chalk, his lips rouged so that he looked as pretty as any geisha, and he began to sing in a lilting falsetto.

O what am I to do?
I'm such a lonely girl.
A poppy in a paddy field.
All around me are weeds
Which choke and stifle me.
O what am I to do
I'm such a lonely girl!

As Ito sang Hayama leant across and whispered in Strickland's ear, giving a brief outline of the play 'The Gilded Cage', which was an old favourite in Japan. The story was about a beautiful young woman called Sweet Pea who is married to a wealthy but hopeless drunk and is obliged to take lovers because her husband ignores her. Ito stopped singing and the chorus began.

Poor little city girl
As fragrant and pretty as a rose.
She lives out in the country
Surrounded by rustics.
Poor little city girl,
Married to a drunken bore
Who spends all his money
On sake and gambles.
He doesn't deserve her.
Poor little city girl!

A burly man arrived on stage staggering and carrying a flagon, which he waved about his head. Despite the actor's beard and make-up, Strickland could see that it was Sergeant Noguchi and the chorus began to sing again.

Here he comes now!
Look at him, as drunk as ten men.
What a hopeless slob!
Full of grand gestures

And empty promises.
Wait till he gets into bed.
He'll wilt like a geranium
You'll see!
He'll wilt like a geranium
You'll see!

The husband began to sing, his 'basso profundo' voice rumbling like a storm cloud as it filled the mess hall.

I am a rather splendid fellow,
It's true.
As lithe and supple as an athlete
And as fecund as a bull.
O come to bed my jasmine blossom,
Your skin's as pale as moonlight.
O come to bed my ocean pearl,
Your eyes shine like the stars!

Sweet Pea stopped brushing her hair and taking her husband's hand to great whistles and catcalls from the audience, she drew back the covers and the pair of them got into bed. As soon as the sergeant's head hit the pillow he gave an enormous belch and began to snore and the chorus burst into song once more.

He's a slob, he's an oaf.
He's got a belly full of sake
And a radish in his trousers!
O what's a woman to do?
O what's a woman to do?

The heroine then sat up in bed, sounding forlorn as she sang.

While the birds make their nests
And fill them with their young

My bower is empty and silent.
Like a petrel tossed on a stormy sea,
How I long for a proper home!

And so Sweet Pea was left with no other choice but to take a succession of lovers, hiding them under the bed or getting them to jump out of the window when her husband arrived home drunk and bellowing and demanding satisfaction which he could never give. The audience roared with laughter and cheered as the cuckold began to suspect that something was awry, but of course could never catch the perpetrators. The climax came when the husband failed to come home one night and Sweet Pea discovered that he had been so drunk, he had fallen down a well and drowned. She went through the motions of mourning and wearing widow's weeds, but in a dramatic finale she stripped them off, returning to the city a free woman. The chorus rose and sang a rousing finish.

The nightingale has fled
Her gilded cage
And taken to the air.
How sweet the taste
Of freedom is!
How sweet the taste
Of freedom is!

The curtain fell and when it was raised again, the cast came forward for their bow. Hayama and Strickland stood and applauded, along with the rest of the soldiers who shouted and stamped their feet. The cheers grew as Sergeant Noguchi emerged from the wings to take his turn and rose in a crescendo when Ito appeared. The orderly smiled happily as the soldiers whistled and pounded the floor with their boots. It had been a virtuoso performance and with the applause reverberating around the hall, the rest of the cast pushed him to the front of the stage and began to clap as well. Ito stood there and took another bow as the audience cheered him on. He looked at the two officers who were shouting and clapping as loudly as anyone and smiled shyly and bowed. The orderly had been the star of the show.

After several encores the cast departed from the stage and the audience began to disperse. Hayama and Strickland left the mess and wandered out into the night air, the sound of applause still ringing in their ears. They walked across the compound without a word, neither man wanting to break the spell. A nightjar called like a voice from the underworld. The officers stopped and listened to the bird's solitary song. What was it saying? It sounded like a warning. But a warning of what? The nightjar's chirring grew fainter and fainter, until there was only silence. The two friends walked on, above them cold fires burned in the heavens. The air was pure and still and a mist rose from the full moon.

SEVEN

The submarine slid through the black waters of the harbour like an eel through marshland, the engines making a low humming noise. On its conning tower the letters I-47 gleamed palely in the moonlight. A bow wave rippled and shone like mercury as the vessel made its way towards the jetty, a trail of phosphorescence floating in its wake. Inside the darkened hull of the vessel Commander Kazuo Shimura was standing knee deep in water, encouraging his men as they continued to work the pumps by hand. The electrics had been destroyed in the attack and the only light inside the vessel came from the open hatch of the conning tower. Inside, it was foul and reeked of diesel and sweat, as Shimura gazed upwards, feeling the night air press against his face. He looked down and saw his men working away as they kept the submarine afloat, many of them stripped naked because of the heat, their bodies covered in grease and engine oil. They were safe now they had reached the island. But the day before had been very different. At dawn they had attacked an American convoy, torpedoing a merchant ship before the escorting destroyers were alerted and began to hunt them down. They had been depth charged so many times that Shimura had lost count. Each explosion had rocked the vessel until it seemed the hull would crack open like an egg. Somehow they had survived and finally evading the escorts, I-47 had slipped away.

A whistle blew and taking the communication pipe, the commander put it to his ear and ordered the engines to be stilled. He replaced the pipe and ascended the conning tower's iron ladder, joining his second in command who had been acting as the pilot, guiding the submarine through the reef.

'We're here, sir,' said the lieutenant, standing to attention and saluting his superior officer as he appeared on the bridge.

'Nice work, Yoshida,' replied his commander and looking out over the parapet, he watched as his men emerged from the forward hatch and secured the vessel to the pier with steel hawsers. When they had finished Shimura took the communication pipe and ordered the rest of his crew out from the submarine. He replaced the pipe and climbing down the conning tower, the commander joined his company on the quayside. Yoshida followed him and listened as Shimura congratulated his men on their work and explained how their discipline and training had saved their lives. He told the company to go and get some rest, they would begin repairs at dawn.

The commander turned to his lieutenant and looked at his exhausted, oil-smeared face and smiled.

'That includes you, Yoshida.'

'What about you, sir? You must rest too.'

'I will, but first I must go and see Captain Hayama and tell him what has happened.'

Yoshida saluted his commander and watched as he turned and strode away down the jetty. The lieutenant waited until he had gone before addressing the submarine's company again. He repeated Shimura's orders and telling them to fall out, he leant against a wooden pile and took out a packet of cigarettes from the pocket of his tunic. The cigarettes were damp and smelt of diesel, but Yoshida managed to light one and as he inhaled all the tension and fear he felt evaporated and his heart was light as he gazed up at the ghost moon.

Strickland was startled awake by a hand shaking his shoulder.

'Quick! You must get up and leave!' said a voice in the darkness.

The pilot opened his eyes and tried to find the voice's face. The room was swathed in black and he could see only a dim shape. He knew the voice belonged to Ito, but why had he come to wake him in the middle of the night?

'What is it, Ito? What's happened?'

'The submarine has returned! You must leave now. Come quickly!'

The pilot leapt out of bed and putting on his clothes and sandals he followed Ito, slipping out the back of the hut and into the yard. In the distance he could hear the sound of engines throbbing and through the trees he saw the dark outline of the submarine as it made its way across the harbour.

'Here, take this!' said the orderly, thrusting a canvas bag into the pilot's hands. 'It's some food, enough for three days at least. A week if you're careful. You must move only at night. Do not come anywhere near the camp.'

'And Hayama?'

'He knows. Quick! You must go!'

The pilot dashed off into the undergrowth, the lianas and branches swatting his face and arms as he stumbled over the great roots of the banyans that blocked his flight. He found the path that led towards the mountain and continued headlong up the incline, frantic for breath, his lungs heaving as he ran. Before the forest petered out into the plantains and banks of elephant grass, Strickland turned away from the path and forded the stream that flowed down the mountain, his feet slipping upon the moss-strewn rocks as he splashed his way to the other side. He reached the bank and gasping, looked about.

Up ahead there was a spinny of young trees and he crawled into the middle of the thicket, dragging the bag of food after him. He settled down in the pitch darkness, surrounded by dense scrub and listened as his breath came in shallow, painful rasps. There was nothing, just the faint music of the stream as it fell towards the sea. The pilot could smell the leaves and dry earth beneath him and knew that no rain or sunlight ever penetrated this place. He was safe from prying eyes. Gradually his breath and sense of equilibrium returned and using the bag as a pillow, Strickland lay down to rest. He looked up at the dark and heavy foliage which hung above his head and wondered why the submarine had returned, and thought that perhaps he had been betrayed.

Yet Ito had told him to flee and said that Hayama knew, so it could not be. Once again the captain had saved the pilot's life. How could he ever repay his debt? He realised there had to be a reason for the submarine's return, but whatever it was he must stay hidden for as long as the vessel remained at the island. Strickland lay cocooned in the undergrowth, listening to the forest sounds and the distant song of the stream as it cascaded over the rocks. He felt secure in his hiding place and hoped Hayama would not worry. It was only now that he understood the extraordinary risk the captain had taken in sparing his life. This singular act of compassion had so surprised the pilot that he had never given it any further thought. It would have been so much easier for the captain if he had executed him and yet he had not. He had said himself that he did not know why. It was fate which had decreed it should be so and Hayama the faithful servant had obeyed. Strickland also knew that one day the gods would demand their dues and he would have to repay his debt.

The captain sat at his desk chain smoking, bathed in the light of a solitary lamp as he waited for the submarine's commander to arrive. He had already sent Noguchi down to the harbour to greet Shimura, lest he should think it strange that a man of subordinate rank had not bothered to do so himself. Hayama had been concerned the Englishman might have been tempted to give himself up out of some erroneous sense of honour and that would have been disastrous for everyone. So, he had stayed behind just in case, until Ito had told him that all was well and the pilot had disappeared into the forest.

Hayama tried to relax, but the tension he felt within was almost overwhelming. His hand shook as he held his cigarette. He put it to his lips and drew deeply on the filter, exhaling a cloud of smoke which swam in the pool of light before him, slowly dissipating into the night air. He heard the sound of foot-steps approaching and stubbing out his cigarette, he got to his feet. The captain straightened his uniform and saw two figures ascend the stairs and appear at his doorway.

The sergeant walked into the room and bowing low at Hayama, he introduced his visitor.

'Commander Shimura-san of the Combined Fleet honours us with his presence, sir.'

'Indeed we are honoured,' replied Hayama with a bow. 'You are most welcome.'

Shimura gave a curt salute and stepping forward, he extended a hand in greeting. Hayama took it and offered his superior the chair opposite his desk and they sat down.

'Will that be all, sir?' asked Noguchi standing at the doorway.

'Yes, thank you,' replied the captain and with another bow, the sergeant turned and left.

For a moment the Japanese officers looked at each other and the contrast could hardly have been more different. Hayama neatly turned out as always, his khaki uniform spotless, his boots well polished. Whereas the submariner was covered in grease and engine oil and had the sour vinegar smell of someone who has not washed in weeks. Shimura's face was filthy and beneath the dirt you could see the stress and exhaustion etched in the lines of his face. Years of patrolling under the surface of the sea and attacking and evading enemy shipping had taken their toll. His eyes had a dark and hooded look about them like a crow's.

'Would you care for some refreshment, commander?'

'Yes ... please.'

The captain called out to his orderly to bring them some tea and as they waited he offered his guest a cigarette, which he declined.

'I'm sorry I forgot. You don't smoke. You don't mind if I do?'

Shimura shook his head and watched as his host lit yet another Kinshi, his fingers trembling slightly.

'I apologise for my unexpected return, captain, but it was

absolutely necessary. I couldn't inform you because I didn't want to break radio silence, in case we were still being pursued by the enemy.'

'There's no need to explain yourself, commander. I quite understand. I'm simply glad that you are safe and well.'

Shimura nodded and looking up he saw Ito emerge from the kitchen with a tray, which the orderly put down on the desk in front of them. He departed and the captain began to pour them both some tea. On a plate were some sweet rice cakes known as *omochi*, which he offered to his superior. Shimura took one and together the two men drank their jasmine tea, Hayama's cigarette smoke trailing through the humid air.

The captain listened as the commander told him of his successful attack on the American convoy and their fortunate escape, adding that their hull had been badly damaged during the destroyers' subsequent pursuit and would take several days to repair.

'I'm glad the gods have smiled upon your endeavour and that you will soon be able to continue your glorious work against the enemy. Naturally my men are at your disposal. If there is anything else you require, you only have to ask.'

Shimura smiled and drained his cup and Hayama dutifully refilled it and offered him another rice cake which he accepted. The captain took a last drag of his cigarette and stubbed it out in the ashtray, before picking up his packet and lighting another. He took a deep drag and exhaling, he began filling his own cup. The commander noticed the teapot tremble briefly in his grasp, and put it down to exhaustion. He was tired enough himself.

The submariner looked at his watch and stifled a yawn with his hand. There were only a couple of hours left until dawn.

'If you don't mind, captain, I would like to get some rest. I have told my men they are to start repairs at first light and I want to oversee the operation.'

'Of course,' replied his subordinate. 'There is an empty quarter next to mine. You can use that.'

The officers drained their cups of tea and stood up. Hayama led the way and leaving his own hut, he ascended the steps of the one next door. He opened the fly screen and stepped inside, Shimura following him. The place was dark and the captain went over to the bed and taking out his cigarette lighter, he lit the hurricane lamp on the table, the flame casting an amber glow around the cabin.

'This will be fine,' said the commander, oberving his surroundings. It had been a long time since he had slept in a cot on dry land. He looked across at the shelf by the bed and saw Ensign Aoki's photograph.

'A previous occupant?'

The captain nodded and explained how his second in command had succumbed to a fever during the last monsoon.

'Most unfortunate. And these?' he asked, picking up a set of dog tags which lay beside the picture. 'Are they his?'

If Shimura had not had his back to him, he would have seen Hayama turn as white as a geisha. The commander flipped the tags over in his hand and examined them.

'No ... they are not. They are in English ...' and he held them out, the metal gleaming dully in the light.

'They belonged to the pilot you shot down,' said the captain. 'His body washed up on the shore. I took his identity tags because I thought I might send them to his family. I must have left them here by mistake. I wondered where they had got to,' and reaching out he took the metal discs and put them in his pocket.

Shimura observed his subordinate and realised that he was lying. He did not know how he knew this, he just did. Perhaps it was his years as a submariner, living with men at close quarters. He knew his crew intimately. More importantly, he could always tell when someone was not telling him the truth. There were no secrets aboard a submarine. The commander wondered why the captain should want to lie. Part of what he said, he knew was correct. He had seen the aircraft crash into the sea with his own eyes and he doubted the pilot could have survived the impact. He may have been dead already. Yet he could be mistaken. Perhaps the pilot had survived. Whatever had happened, it was unlikely that he had simply washed up on the beach. The man had been too far out and the current flowed away from the island. Besides, the sharks would have got him long before.

'I see,' said the commander, scrutinising his subordinate.

'It'll be dawn soon,' countered Hayama, avoiding his gaze. 'I'll come and wake you.'

'Thank you,' Shimura replied and acknowledging the captain's brief bow, he watched him leave.

When Hayama had gone the commander went to the shelf where the dog tags had been. On it was the ensign's photograph. Shimura looked at the face staring impassively out at him.

'You see everything, but you cannot speak,' he said.

The commander turned away and began to undress. He put his oil-smeared clothes on a chair and pulling aside the mosquito net, he got into bed. The submariner blew out the lamp and as he lay there in the darkness, he wondered about Hayama. Why had the captain lied to him about the identity tags? And if he had lied, which he was sure he had, what had happened to the pilot? Was he on the island? And if he was, then where was he? It just did not make sense. Shimura closed his eyes. He was too tired to think clearly. His recent ordeal had exhausted him and glad of the respite and the comfort of a bed, he quickly fell asleep.

EIGHT

Dawn broke over the island, casting shadows across the mountain, the sea's dark stain diminishing as night fell from the heavens and the stars extinguished their fires. As the light increased the sun rose like a nymph from the deep, naked and tender as a newborn, flames flickering and falling from her shoulders in a burning watery garment, the sea coiling and writhing like a serpent beneath her feet. On the island a mist rose from the forest as dew evaporated in the heat, trailing an ethereal hand across the green canopy. Among the trees birds sang, the forest reverberating to their cries as they filled the air with their voices. As the birds chorused, the rest of the island awoke and a new day began.

The pilot lay hidden in the depths of the undergrowth, listening to the sounds of the forest as the sun rose above the treetops. Nearby he heard the sound of scratching and turning his head, he saw a jungle fowl pecking and scraping at the dirt. He lay still, the bird unaware as it foraged for insects among the fallen leaves. The jungle fowl continued its quest and moved away, leaving Strickland alone in his bower. He sat up and reached for the bag behind him, opening it to see what Ito had provided. He emptied the contents into his lap and an array of neatly wrapped parcels fell out. There was also a water bottle and the pilot unscrewed the cap and drank. He replaced the top and began unwrapping the parcels of food. There were fillets of salted fish, some rice balls, a handful of green beans, some limes and a fresh papaya. Enough to keep him going for several days, if he was careful.

Strickland peeled the papaya and ate half of the fruit, putting the rest of it back in the leaf that had wrapped it. He then ate a couple of the rice balls and washed them down with some more water from his canteen. The pilot replaced the remaining food in the bag and put it to one side. With his eyes accustomed to the gloom, he looked about his bower and realised that he could not have picked a better hiding place. He was a long way from the camp and a fair distance from the mountain path. In order to find his hideout someone would have to come looking for him with dogs.

As the Englishman sat alone in his forest cell he felt the solitude of a hermit and his thoughts turned once again to the little friar. Although Fray Juan had been incarcerated in a bare room with only a single window high up in the wall, he had used his period of isolation for his own enlightenment. Strickland thought it would be a good exercise for him to try and remember in detail everything that he had learned about the saint, to see if he could retrieve the man's writings and poetry from the recesses of his memory. It would occupy the hours and he would have something to tell Hayama when he next saw him. The captain admired the friar and always wanted to know more. It was as if John's own example of self-abnegation and compassion had blown upon some ashes that lay deep within the captain's soul and kindled a fire within. As the mystic himself had written: '*And when the Divine fire has transformed the substance of the soul into itself, not only is the soul conscious of the burn, but it has itself become one burn of vehement fire.*'

And yet the more that the pilot discovered about Hayama's faith, the more he was captivated by the philosophy of reincarnation; being constantly reborn until such a state of grace was obtained that man became a Buddha. It seemed as though reincarnation was the oriental version of purgatory, that life had to be lived again and the soul cleansed until it was pure.

There was also 'karma', a word Strickland had first heard about from the captain, who explained that every desire and action has a necessary reaction. Just as a pebble thrown into a pond made ripples, so whatever a person did also entailed a consequence.

Yet karma was not only a tenet of Buddhism, but also of Christianity. St Paul had said precisely this in his letter to the Galatians when he wrote, '*whatever a man sows, he shall reap.*' The different faiths had many aspects that complimented each other. They were like two halves of the same fruit and in the middle were the pips, the seeds of faith. The pilot wondered what John the mystic would have made of the contemplative Buddhist life and was sure that it was not so very different from his own.

In John's work 'Living Flame' Strickland remembered how the friar had described the Holy Spirit as penetrating '*the soul continually, deifying its substance and making it Divine*' and as absorbing '*the soul, above all being, in the Being of God.*' Such insights appeared in Christian metaphors used by mystics for their descriptions of divine union: the twin candle flames, the window and the ray of sunlight, the log burning in the fire. All of these images were continually used by John and none of them implied a loss of personality, except that the log was eventually united with the fire and became '*one living flame within it.*' Again this echoed Buddhism's own pantheistic imagery of salt dissolving in water and rivers flowing into the ocean.

The pilot was glad his memory served him well and thought the captain would be pleased to know about this latest juxtaposition of their faiths. He sat back against the narrow boughs of the spinney and closed his eyes. He was exhausted after his dash up the mountain in the middle of the night. His mind turned to the concert party and the orderly dressed as Sweet Pea singing her songs, and he smiled to himself. Strickland had always been comfortable with Hayama and Ito. Now he felt that he had been accepted by the rest of the camp. He was no longer an outsider, but a companion. And yet, while the pilot trusted Hayama's men implicitly, he knew he was not safe so long as the submarine and its crew were on the island.

The Englishman remained in his self-imposed purdah for the next three days, venturing outside only after dark in order to stretch his legs and gaze at the stars. He would stand beside the spinney looking up at the full moon as it hung like a lantern in the heavens. Later, Strickland would go down to the stream and fill his canteen, which would last him for another day. After drawing in a last few draughts of the night air, he would return to the dim recess of his hiding place.

On the fourth day, the pilot was eating breakfast in his bower when his foot knocked over his water bottle, spilling the contents onto the ground. He cursed quietly and picked it up, but there was barely a drop left. Strickland looked at the patch of damp earth and wondered whether he should risk going out to refill it. He decided to wait until dusk, when the men stopped work and gathered for their evening meal. It was unlikely anyone would venture up the mountain at that time. It also meant he would not have to go out in the middle of the night. Besides, the pilot had become confident about his hiding place and had not seen, nor heard of anyone since his arrival. There was also another reason why he wanted to leave his bower while it was still light. A large mango tree grew nearby, whose fruit was beginning to ripen. The pilot had finished his papaya and limes and with only salted fish and a few rice balls left, he yearned for something sweet. It would only take a moment to climb the tree and pick some fruit.

As the evening sun lowered in the sky, Strickland crept out from his bower. He waited by a rock and listened. Except for the low murmur of water and the occasional cry from a troop of monkeys, there was silence. He crept down the mountain path towards the mango, treading softly as he went. He spied the tree a short way off, its branches framed by the light of the descending sun. The pilot looked about and saw that everything was quiet, and approaching the tree he grabbed a branch and began to climb. The mango's leaves rustled and shook as the Englishman shinned up the bough, the cloying smell of fruit assailing his nostrils. He reached the canopy where the mangoes were the ripest and holding onto a branch with his left hand, he selected one burnished by the sun, which he plucked and put inside his shirt. Strickland had just picked another and was about to descend, when he heard the sounds of footfall and the voice of someone singing. His heart jolted in his chest and peering down, he saw an elderly Japanese sailor walking up the trail. The pilot's concern turned to consternation when the sailor left the path and began to walk straight towards him. The crewman reached the tree, but did not look up. Instead, he sat down at its base and took out a packet of cigarettes. He struck a match and lit one, the smoke drifting away on the evening air.

The pilot remained hidden in the upper branches of the mango, praying the man would not see him. The old sailor took his time enjoying his cigarette and admiring the view from the mountain. He was so close Strickland could see the lines of his face, the man squinting as he looked at the setting sun. With a sigh the sailor finally stubbed out his cigarette on a rock. It was time to return to the submarine. He got to his feet and was about to leave when he spotted a mango on the ground. He took it, sniffed the fruit and smiled. He would share it later with his crewmates. Then the crewman looked up into the tree to see if any others were ripe and his eyes widened in disbelief when he saw a bedraggled, blond-haired man staring at him. Whoever it was, he certainly was not Japanese and the sailor dropped the mango and bolted towards the path.

Strickland jumped down and landing on all fours, he sprang after the sailor as he disappeared through the trees. The crewman ran quickly, but he was not as young or as fit as the pilot, who soon gained on him. A moment later the Englishman caught up and tackling him, they both fell to the ground. The sailor cried out in fear and put up a tremendous struggle, as the pilot wrestled with him in the dirt.

'*Tomare!*' Strickland shouted, as the man thrashed and wriggled beneath him like a trapped eel. '*Tomadachi! Tomadachi!*' he repeated.

'*Iie! Iie! Iie!*' cried the crewman, refusing to give up.

The men continued their desperate struggle, with neither

gaining the upper hand. The sailor managed to slip partly from the pilot's grasp and reaching down, he pulled his bayonet from its scabbard and struck his adversary on the side of the head. Before he could deal another blow Strickland grabbed his hand, the bright blade inches from his face. The bayonet shook before his eyes as they remained locked in their deadly clutch. With both hands grasping the hilt, Strickland gradually drew the knife away from his face and forced it down towards the man's chest. With a final effort, he plunged it deep between his ribs. He twisted the knife and the crewman quivered like a stricken animal, his grip on the bayonet loosening as his life ebbed away. The pilot held him tightly in a dying embrace, the man's eyes looking directly into his. The sailor almost smiled at him before his body went slack, the light in his eyes fading into infinity.

Strickland rolled away exhausted, his energy sapped by the fight. His breath came in thin rasps and he sucked air down into his lungs. His body was covered in sweat and his limbs shook from exertion. As his breath returned he got to his knees and looked at the body which lay beside him. The man was quite still, his eyes staring blankly at the sky. The pilot remembered that look. He had seen it before, a long time ago. When he was a boy he had once shot a blackbird with an air rifle, while it sang in the branches of a rowan. As the dying bird lay at his feet, it had the same look in its eyes. The look of death. Strickland did not know why he had killed the bird and confronted with his childish crime, he had stood there and wept. He never told anyone and buried the bird secretly in the rose garden. Now he had done something far worse and he felt sick. The Englishman turned away and feeling a sudden surge in the pit of his stomach, he vomited into the long grass.

The pilot stood up and wiping away the bitter taste of bile from his mouth, he looked at the corpse beside him. The sun had left the sky and the shadows lengthened. Soon it would be dark. Strickland wondered what he should do with the body. He could not leave it here and yet he did not want to take it back to his hiding place. The idea of sleeping next to a dead man was abhorrent and besides the body would soon begin to smell. It could be several more days before the submarine left and they were bound to come looking for the sailor. He had to hide the body where it would never be found. The pilot thought he knew of such a place and putting his arms under the man's shoulders, he began to drag the crewman back along the path.

By the time Strickland reached the ravine it was dark. The constellations were scattered in a brilliant dust across the heavens and the moon glimmered coldly like a coin in a fountain. The pilot heaved the sailor's corpse towards the edge of the escarpment, his limbs aching from the effort. The cliff was covered by thick scrub, so that it was impossible to see down into the gulley. Strickland picked up a stone, threw it in and listened, hearing its dull echo as it struck the rocky floor below. It was deep enough and hauling the corpse to its feet, he pitched the dead man head first into the ravine. There was a rushing sound as the body plummeted through the fringe of thorn, followed by a low thud as it hit the bottom of the crevasse.

The pilot made his way back to his hideout, stopping briefly to fill his canteen in the stream. He crossed over to the far bank and getting on his hands and knees, he crawled through the spinney and into his bower. He sat there in the darkness, listening to the sounds of the stream as it burbled away. Strickland knew the submarine's company would come looking for the crewman. He was sure they would never find the body and he doubted they would ever find him. Yet how would Hayama explain the sailor's disappearence? His eyes searched the impenetrable gloom vainly seeking solace, but there was none. The pilot had never felt so desperate and so alone, and clasping his hands before him, he prayed to the little friar.

NINE

Hayama was sitting cross-legged on the tatami eating his breakfast when the door of his hut burst open, and looking up he saw Shimura standing there with his feet apart, his face dark with rage.

'One of my men is missing!' he barked. 'He went for a walk after supper and has not returned. I want to know why!'

The captain looked at him perplexed and indicated that he should sit down.

'Please calm yourself, commander. I'm sure there is a proper explanation. Won't you have some breakfast?'

Shimura glared at him and shook his head. Curled up asleep in the captain's lap was a young macaque. What sort of man, he wondered, kept a monkey for a pet?

'There isn't time! The submarine is repaired and we're ready to leave. We must organise a search party!'

'Of course,' replied Hayama and putting Chamberlain back in his box, he rinsed his fingers in a bowl of water and led the commander outside. He called out to one of his men and told him to go and fetch Noguchi. The man ran off to the mess hall and when the NCO appeared he explained what had happened. The captain told him to assemble the men in the square and to bring the submarine's company as well. The sergeant bowed and saluted the officers and went off to carry out his orders.

Standing on the porch, Hayama turned and seeing that Shimura was still fuming, he tried to calm him.

'I'm sure there's a reason. Perhaps your man got lost. He'll probably turn up at any moment. Maybe he was drunk.'

The commander observed his subordinate, barely able to disguise his contempt.

'My men never drink on patrol,' he said and he looked away across the compound, his gaze ascending the mountain that rose above the forest. 'I know he's out there somewhere ...' he muttered.

The officers waited in silence as their men arrived and gathered in the sunlit square. When they had all lined up, Shimura addressed them.

'As some of you already know, yesterday evening one of my crewmen went for a walk in the forest and did not come back. We must look for him. No leaf or stone should be left unturned. He may have hurt himself and be unable to move, so make plenty of noise so that he can hear you. Since Captain Hayama's men know the island and we do not, we will team up with them.'

The commander faced his subordinate.

'It's up to you how you conduct the search. But we had better find him.'

Hayama nodded and began to address the assembled men. They would fan out in a line and sweep the island like a broom, starting from the beach and working their way up the mountain. He and Commander Shimura would lead the way. The men then fell out and walked in single file down to the shore led by their officers, and the search party spread out across the beach. At a singal from Hayama they returned through the trees and passing the camp, headed on up the mountain. As the men searched they shouted and whistled, calling out the sailor's name so that the forest was filled with cries and disembodied voices, as if a company of ghosts had descended upon the island.

Hidden deep within the spinney, Strickland heard them approaching and listened as they called out and beat the bushes in their path. He lay quite still and waited as a patrol forded the stream and walked right by his hiding place. He held his breath, but they did not look into the spinney and continued on, their voices rising and falling above the rushing water. The pilot knew that even if they found the ravine, they were unlikely to venture down into it. Both he and the dead man were safe.

The day drew on and as evening fell, the search party returned empty-handed and gathered disconsolately back at the camp. The men were exhausted, their arms and faces cut by the branches and lianas of the forest. They did not know that the man they were looking for lay in a perpetual slumber at the bottom of a crevasse, deaf to the sound of their calling. The men assembled in front of Hayama's cabin and the officers stood on the verandah facing them.

Shimura addressed the company and thanked them for their work. It was unfortunate they were unable to find the crewman, he must have had an accident. Whatever had happened they could not spend any more time searching for him. The submarine had a mission to complete and this must be their priority. They would set sail as soon as it got dark. He told his men to fall out and watched as his crew set off to prepare their vessel for the voyage home.

With the square empty, Shimura turned to Hayama.

'I want a word with you, captain,' he said. 'Let's go inside.'

Hayama gave a small bow and they entered his quarters. The commander turned to his subordinate, a look of malice in his dark eyes.

'Tell me the truth about the pilot,' he demanded.

The captain stood there silently. He did not know what to say. He knew the commander suspected something because of the dog tags, but he could not tell him the pilot was on the island. Nor did he know what had happened to the unfortunate sailor. Perhaps there was a perfectly innocent explanation. But he realised he had to say something.

'Commander, I'm so sorry about your missing crewman ...' he began.

'Forget him, he's dead,' hissed Shimura. 'I want to know about the pilot. Where is he?'

'I told you. His body washed up on the shore.'

'Don't lie to me!' spat the commander, his voice rising in anger. 'The current is far too strong, it would have carried him away from the island.'

Hayama did not reply immediately and looked at Shimura. He was an astute man and plainly he suspected something. But apart from the identity tags, he had no evidence. The only thing the captain could do was to keep to his story.

'There was a storm, the waves carried the body into the lagoon.'

'What did you do with the body?'

'We buried it at sea.'

'Why didn't you bury it on the island?'

'Because he was not Japanese.'

'You expect me to believe that?'

'It's what happened.'

'No! I'll tell you what happened. The pilot survived the crash and you rescued him!'

Hayama was speechless. How did Shimura know this? Had one of his men told him? Was he psychic? He did not know what to say and he stood there dumbfounded, staring hopelessly at the commander.

'I'm right, aren't I?' said Shimura, glaring at him.

'Yes, sir, you are,' said a voice.

The officers wheeled round and saw the orderly standing in the corner. He had been preparing supper in the kitchen and had heard everything.

'So, tell me … private?'

'Private Ito, sir.'

'Very well, Private Ito. Please go on.'

Hayama looked aghast at his servant. Had he betrayed them? Inwardly he begged him not to divulge what had happened. It would only make things worse. But the orderly continued.

'The pilot's plane crashed, but before it sank he sent out a distress flare. We had to search for him in case the enemy came looking. If the enemy had found him, he would have told them of our whereabouts and all would have been lost. You would not have been able to return here to repair your vessel …' and Ito paused.

The commander nodded. He was calmer now and wanted to hear what the orderly had to say.

'Please continue.'

'The pilot was in a very bad way. He had been in the water too long. He was almost dead. We took him back here, but he never regained conciousness. He died the next day.'

'If he was in such a bad way, why did you not leave him to the sharks?'

Shimura was looking at the captain.

'I thought he might recover. If he had then he would have given us valuable intelligence about enemy movements in the area. Information that would have been helpful to people like yourself. As it was we learnt nothing,' and Hayama shrugged, the last part of what he said being perfectly true. Strickland had never told them anything during his interrogation.

The commander gave a wintry smile.

'I think you have only told me part of what you know. Both of you. But I suspect something else, something treasonable. Aiding and abetting the enemy is a capital offence. I am going to recommend you for court martial, Captain Hayama. Your men will all be summoned to testify. If found guilty, as I'm sure you will be, you will be sentenced to death.'

Shimura turned and faced the orderly, his deadly eyes fixed upon him like a snake's.

'And you shall be the prosecution's principle witness, Private Ito.'

The submarine commander then donned his cap and without another word, he turned on his heel and walked out of the hut, leaving Hayama and his orderly staring after him.

It was dark when the submarine slipped its moorings and slid out of the harbour, departing as silently as it had come. The vessel sliced through the black waters of the lagoon, its propellers leaving a trail of phosphorescence in its wake. The captain waited alone on the shoreline and saw the solitary figure of Shimura standing in the conning tower, as I-47 made its way towards the reef. The commander did not look back, but continued to gaze straight ahead as the vessel passed through the narrow channel and headed for the open sea, the moonlight reflecting palely off the surf. Hayama watched it go and as the submarine was gradually consumed by the darkness, he felt an overwhelming sense of relief. The island was theirs once again.

TEN

Ito took the path that led up the mountain. He had no idea where Strickland was hidden, but suspected it was somewhere far away from the camp and near running water. That meant he had to be on the mountain. The orderly walked quickly up the trail, pausing now and then to rest and enjoy the early morning sun as it cascaded through the branches of the trees. In the canopy bright plumed birds courted each other, shaking their feathers in a dance. Here and there blue-winged butter-flies flitted among the frangipani and hibiscus, pausing to drink from the forest flowers. Ito passed a glade and stopped to sit on a boulder, watching the insects as they flew here and there among the flowers. They reminded him of the gardens at Dejima island in Nagasaki, the only place in Japan where foreigners had been permitted to trade, and he wondered when he would see them again. As he sat and watched the butterflies, he recited a haiku written centuries ago:

A butterfly
Poised on a tender orchid
How sweetly the incense
Burns on its wings.

The orderly smiled to himself and continued on, leaving the damasked-winged dryads behind. He walked up the trail and passed the mango tree where the sailor had met his nemesis and, turning off the path, he followed the sound of running water until he came to the stream. Ito started to call out the pilot's name, walking along the banks of the water course.

Sitting in his hiding place Strickland heard his friend's voice rising and falling above the rushing water. The pilot crawled out from his bower and stood up. Below him he could see the orderly as he made his way up the stream, stopping now and then to call his name.

'Hey Ito!' he cried. 'I'm over here.'

The orderly turned and screwing up his face he squinted at the rising sun and saw the pilot standing on a boulder waving at him. He smiled, waved back and began to make his way upstream towards the Englishman.

When he got there they hugged each other and laughed, delighted to see one another again.

'Is it safe now?' asked Strickland, breaking from the embrace and grinning at his friend.

'Yes, thanks be to God. The submarine, it went last night. But, oh, we had most difficult time with commander. He lost a man and we search all the island.'

'I know.'

'You saw us?'

'I heard you. A group passed right by my hiding place, just over there.' The pilot indicated the spinney on the other side of the stream.

Strickland looked away. He realised he would have to tell Hayama what had happened at some point. But he did not want to say anything. At least not yet.

'Let's get back to the camp,' he said

As the two men walked down the trail, they passed the spot where the pilot had despatched the sailor. The place bore no trace of their struggle. Instead, sunlight dappled the shadows and the tall grass nodded innocently in the breeze. If it had not actually happened, Strickland would never have believed that this was the place where he had fought and killed a man with his own hands.

The pair continued through the forest, the monkeys chattering in the canopy. They walked past the glade of butterflies and carried on down through the trees, finally arriving back at the camp.

Hayama was sitting at his desk, annotating his notebook. He looked up as his orderly and the pilot entered the hut, his face a mixture of relief and concern. The captain was happy Strickland seemed well and had not been discovered in the search, but they also had much to talk about.

The Japanese officer got to his feet and they shook hands.

'I'm glad to see you,' said Hayama, observing his friend who seemed none the worse for his escapade.

'Me too,' replied Strickland.

'Let's have some tea.' The captain turned to his orderly, who bowed and went off to the kitchen.

'Take a seat,' he said, indicating the empty chair at his desk. The pilot did so and Hayama also sat down.

'I presume Ito told you what happened while you were away.'

'Yes he did. I'm sorry.'

Hayama nodded, a look of resignation on his face.

'Well … there was a problem,' and reaching into his tunic pocket, he pulled out the pilot's dog tags and placed them on the desk in front of him. 'You left these behind.'

The Englishman picked them up and shook his head.

'I haven't worn them in weeks. I'd completely forgotten.'

'The submarine commander found them in your quarters. He was immediately suspicious, but I told him your body had washed up on the shore and that I had removed the tags myself. He didn't believe me, but he didn't have any other choice. Until one of his men went missing …'

The captain paused as a rattle of china indicated the orderly's return. Ito emerged with a tray bearing cups and a teapot and setting it down on the desk, he departed again. Hayama picked up the pot and poured them both a cup and the officers sat there in silence drinking their tea.

The captain continued sipping his drink, observing the pilot. Eventually he spoke.

'I don't suppose you are able to … shed any light on this?'

'Actually I can,' answered Strickland, replacing his cup and looking directly at his friend. 'I killed him.'

'What!' Hayama spluttered, tea spraying his uniform. 'Are you quite mad?'

'He saw me picking mangoes.'

'Why on earth were you out picking mangoes?'

'It was stupid I know, but …'

'But what? You didn't have to kill him!'

Strickland looked at the captain, whose face was flushed with anger. He felt his own blood rising and tried to remain calm.

'I had no choice.'

'What do you mean you had no choice?'

'He ran away! I couldn't let him escape. I had to catch him and when I did, he tried to kill me!'

Hayama let out a long sigh.

'So where's the body?'

'At the bottom of a ravine. I made sure no one would be able to find it.'

The captain pushed his cup aside and shook his head sadly. He never imagined something like this might happen. He wondered if the gods were punishing him for some act or failing, which he could not recall. If he had angered them in some way, they were exacting a heavy price.

'Why? Why did this have to happen?' he muttered, raising his eyes to the roofbeams.

Neither man spoke and they sat there in silence, both simmering with resentment. The only sound was the incessant calling of the cicadas in the trees outside, an unending chorus of accusation.

Amid the mad cacophony an idea came to the pilot, which he thought offered a solution to their predicament.

'Hayama … I'm grateful for all that you've done for me. I know I owe you a debt I cannot repay …' and Strickland hesitated, trying to find the right words. 'It's dangerous me being here on the island. This could easily happen again. You have your own men to consider.'

The captain frowned at him.

'What are you suggesting?'

'I think that I should leave.'

'What? Leave the island?'

'Yes.'

'How?'

'The patrol boat has a dinghy. I could use that. There are plenty of Allied forces in the area. It wouldn't be long before I was picked up.'

The captain waved a hand dismissively as though brushing away a fly and for the first time since their meeting a smile passed across his face.

'You really are crazy! Don't be absurd. The sea is far too treacherous. The first big wave would flip you over and that would be it.'

'But the submarine commander knows I'm here, he'll report back to his superiors and someone will come looking.'

'I very much doubt anyone will come looking for you and besides that's the least of my troubles.'

'What do you mean?'

The captain sighed wearily and laid his hands upon the desk, his fingers lightly drumming upon the surface. There was no need to tell the pilot about the court martial.

'It doesn't matter. What's done is done.'

'Hayama, let me take my chances. It would be better that way.'

'Absolutely not. I forbid it!'

The captain looked at his friend. He was brave and selfless to suggest such a thing, but he would not allow him to throw his life away. Yet there was another reason why Hayama would not permit it. He realised their destinies were now so closely entwined, as to be inseparable. The gods had brought the pilot to the island and their fates were inextricably bound together. Only a catastrophic rupture could ever break such a bond.

The officers sat there knowing the storm between them had

passed. It had happened and it was unfortunate, but their friendship had survived the ordeal and their souls were now forged together like the steel of a samurai's sword. Whatever the gods decreed, they would face it together.

ELEVEN

The afternoon sun shone high above the signals hut as the wireless operators sat at the control desk chatting about home and listening to Radio Tokyo. The music of Iva Toguri, better known as Tokyo Rose, filled the airwaves; her siren song drifting through the ether like some heavenly perfume. To Corporal Higa her voice was like a nightingale's, natural and unadorned. It was enough to make a man weep and yet you could not tear yourself away from it, so exquisite was the sense of longing it engendered. As the sound of Tokyo Rose's melodious singing filled the cabin, another more urgent note came from the wireless set.

Higa swung around in his seat and clamping a set of earphones to his head, he began to jot down the morse code that came through. The message was repeated and the corporal checked it against his original draft to make sure that he had not missed anything. The communiqué began and ended with Osaka's own call sign, so he knew that it was genuine and not American propaganda.

It had taken less than a minute for the message to come through and when it finished, Tokyo Rose was still singing the same song.

'Is it serious?' asked Private Kamiko, who had heard Osaka's call sign, but not the communication itself.

'Yes,' answered his fellow operator. 'I must inform the captain at once.'

Higa took off the earphones and left the signals hut, dashing up the path that led towards the bluff above the harbour. He went over the hill and continued down through the forest, the sheet of paper in his hand flapping in the breeze. Running across the sand he made his way towards the camp and passing the pilot's cabin, Higa leapt up the steps of the captain's quarters.

He saw Hayama at his desk and rapping briefly on the fly screen, he entered the hut and bowed. The captain looked quizically at him. It was most unusual for him to be disturbed at this hour, but he could see from the signaller's face that something important must have happened.

'What is it, corporal?' he asked, noticing the man held a scrap of paper in his hand.

'An urgent communiqué from Osaka, captain,' answered his subordinate, breathless from his exertion. 'I thought you should see it immediately.'

Hayama nodded and beckoned the man to come forward. The signaller advanced towards him with the communiqué in his hand. The captain took the note, read it and then he read it again, before shaking his head slowly. He put the sheet of paper down and sitting back in his chair, he ran a hand through his hair.

'Thank you,' he said.

'Will that be all, sir?'

'Yes ... for the time being. I'll make my usual report this evening. If you hear anything else you must tell me at once.'

'Yes, sir,' answered the corporal and bowing again, he left the hut.

Hayama looked down at the piece of paper on his desk and picking it up, he read it once more.

Osaka prefecture reports with great sorrow that His Imperial Majesty's submarine I-47 has been lost with all hands as a result of enemy action. Long live the Emperor!

The captain sat there staring at the words of the communiqué. All those fine young men drowned. He hoped the end had been quick and they had not suffered for long. Hayama let the piece of paper fall from his fingers and stared disconsolately out of the window. There would be no court martial now, but that did not make him feel any better. He would rather face a military tribunal and whatever punishment it chose to administer, than have all those men lying at the bottom of the ocean. Nor had he liked Shimura much either, but the man was only doing his duty as a loyal servant of his Imperial Majesty and like the others, he did not deserve such a death.

'So be it,' Hayama sighed, gazing at the forest and the mountain rising beyond. 'So be it.'

TWELVE

The captain sat in his quarters, writing up his latest report on enemy shipping in the vicinity. He still could not quite believe the communiqué he had received the previous day, having come to the conclusion that Shimura and his submarine were indestructible, but the gods had thought otherwise. He could hear Strickland and his orderly chatting in the yard and presumed they were about to go fishing. He had told them about the fate of I-47 and its crew and both men had been affected by the news. There would, he supposed, be other submarines. What would they do then? The captain did not have an answer to that question and knew he would have to take each circumstance as it arose.

He got up from his desk and went to release Chamberlain, who was sitting in a corner. He picked up the macaque and swung the monkey to and fro, while it gripped him with its paws. Although he had become its surrogate parent, Hayama realised that sooner or later he would have to let Chamberlain go. He would miss the monkey, but he knew it would be unfair to keep him as a pet. The macaque's proper place was with its own kind on the island. Hayama was sure the monkey would survive, there was plenty of food in the forest and he was big enough to look after himself. He put Chamberlain down and giving him a pat, he fastened him to his chain again. Then he went over to his bed and picked up a large white net, which stood in the corner. Ito had told him about the glade in the forest and it was time to add to his butterfly collection. Hayama put the net under his arm and taking his specimen box, he left his cabin and walked across the baking compound. The solitary figure strode through the empty camp and disappeared into the forest.

As the captain set off on his butterfly expedition, Strickland and Ito made their way across the beach to the promontory. The pilot with his fishing rod, the orderly with his mask and harpoon.

'What are you going to catch today?' asked the Englishman, as they clambered up the rocks together.

'Crab. We have not had crab for long time. I wanted to catch one for captain-san's birthday, but I could not find one. Today I will go further out by reef. There are nice crab there.'

'They seem rather hard to catch.'

'Yes, they live deep and hide among rock. When I dive I must take big breath. I can only stay down for short time before I need air.'

'Let's hope you get one,' said the pilot as the pair of them approached the massive piece of basalt that jutted out over the water.

'I will, you'll see,' replied Ito with a smile as he hopped down to the shore.

He spat into his mask and rinsed it with seawater, before putting it over his head. He paused briefly on the rocky ledge with his back to the ocean, before jumping in and disappearing beneath the surface. The orderly reappeared moments later, the sunlight reflecting off the mask's visor as he loaded the spear of his harpoon and with a final wave he set off towards the reef, the pale soles of his feet splashing in the surf. Ahead, the wind whipped the tops of the waves as they crashed over the pale barrier, the air reverberating to the surf's roar.

Strickland watched as the orderly swam into deeper water, the reef a jagged white wall beyond. He looked away and releasing the lure from the shaft, he let it swing freely in the breeze, before raising the rod and casting into the sea. The wind buffeted him as he stood astride the boulder and he began to reel the lure in. He wondered if he would have any luck and hoped that he could surprise Ito by catching a big fish like the wahoo. The pilot continued reeling in his line and cast again into the surf, guiding the silvery bait through the clear, shallow water above the wreck. He could see Ito swimming out by the reef, his figure dwarfed by the great rollers which crashed and thundered across the coral beyond. The orderly disappeared beneath a wave and the pilot carried on with his fishing.

After a while Strickland felt a tug at his line and with a tightening in his chest, he knew he had a bite. The bamboo pole flexed and quivered, the tip bending as the fish dived deeper. Strickland gave his quarry more line and let it run, and when it stopped he carefully began to draw it in. Unaware that it was caught, the fish let itself be guided towards the shore, until it was just a few feet from the rocks. The pilot could see it lying in the limpid water beneath him, the lure hanging from its mouth, although he could not make out what type it was, because of the refraction of the waves. As he peered down at his quarry Strickland's shadow fell across the surface, frightening the fish which took off again, the line whizzing out from the reel. The pilot gripped the rod and chastised himself for this lapse of concentration, hoping he would not lose it. He let the line run for several more yards until the fish stopped and he began to play it once more.

By now his quarry was tiring and Strickland slowly drew it in, the reel clicking with each revolution. Soon the fish was within a couple of feet of the shore again. He put the rod down and nimbly descended the rocks to where it lay. The pilot picked up the line and saw he had caught a sea bream, weighing about four pounds. He gathered in the line and the fish struggled as he pulled it out of the water, its scales glittering in the light. The pilot grabbed it and squeezing its mouth open he removed the hook, the fish's gills flaring pink as he did so. With the lure now free he turned the bream over and put it in the string bag, which he had brought with him. He placed the bag in a pool, putting a rock over one end and watched as the fish briefly thrashed about before settling on the bottom.

The pilot climbed back up the boulder, picked up his rod

and began casting into the water. As he did so he looked out towards the reef to see where Ito was. The waves crashed white against the coral and the sunlight flashed upon the water, but he could see no sign of his friend. Then a figure emerged and began swimming towards him. It seemed the orderly had something in his bag and Strickland wondered if he had managed to catch a crab. In a short while Ito reached the shore and climbing out he stood upon the rocks, his brown body glistening in the sun. He removed the bag from his waist, put his hand inside and pulled out a small octopus, its tentacles writhing around his forearm.

'*Tako*,' he said, looking disappointed as he showed his prize to his companion. He turned it inside out and bit it, then dropped it onto the rock. 'I saw big, big crab, then it hide away. But I see where it goes. It think it is safe. I will go back.'

The orderly glanced at the rock pool and saw the fish the pilot had caught. He bent down and inspected it.

'You have caught *tai*,' he said.

'It's not very big,' said Strickland.

'No, it's good. Enough for two.'

'Are you hungry?'

'Only coconut for breakfast. *Tai* make good meal.'

'I'll go and get some wood, you fillet it.'

'*Oke*,' said Ito and putting his hand into the bag, he brought out the sea bream.

He held it up and admired the fish, its body flashing like mica in the sun. Then he turned it over and smashed its head against the rocks, the bream tensing briefly in his hand before going limp. He sat down on the shore and removing his knife from its sheath, he cut along its silver belly and began to gut the fish. The pilot meanwhile searched among the rocks for pieces of driftwood. There was plenty about and soon he had collected an armful. When he returned he saw the bream lying upon the rock, the fish perfectly filleted by the orderly. Strickland built a small fire and taking out his lighter, he put a flame to the tinder. The wood was dry and caught quickly, a pale plume of smoke rising from the flames as the twigs crackled and burned. The pilot waited for the flames to die down. When the wood merely glowed, he picked up two long sticks and handed one to Ito. He skewered his fillet and held it over the embers. The orderly did the same and the fish began to cook, its pink flesh turning white in the heat. After a couple of minutes the pair removed their sticks from the fire and began to eat the fillet with their fingers.

The flesh was hot and lightly smoked, yet still retained a taste of the sea. Soon the fish was gone and as the embers burned low, the pair sat back against the rocks.

'*Tai* is good fish. It has much flavour,' said the orderly, licking his fingers.

'Yes,' agreed the pilot. 'It was excellent.'

'But *kani* even better. Tonight we will eat *kani*. The captain will be happy.'

'I hope you catch one.'

'Perhaps I catch two.'

Strickland smiled, the orderly was irrepressible.

'You do that. I'm going to have a rest,' he replied, feeling sleepy as the food settled in his stomach. He stretched out on the rocks, closed his eyes and turned his face towards the midday sun.

'See you later,' said Ito as he got to his feet and put his mask back on. He picked up his harpoon and the pilot heard a splash as he jumped into the water. He raised his head, opened one eye and saw the orderly swimming away, then he lay back again. The sun was hot and the sea air soporific so that in a few moments he fell asleep, the surf a disant roaring in his ears.

Strickland slept for some time stretched out like Icarus on the rocks, the wind fingering his hair as the waves lapped the shore below. He woke briefly when a cloud passed across the face of the sun and the air cooled. He propped himself up on an elbow and shading his brow with a hand, he searched the sea for any sign of the orderly, but saw only the light-filled waves shifting beneath the heavens. He lay back and began to doze and had almost fallen asleep again when he heard the most awful scream coming across the water. It was followed by another piercing shriek, high-pitched like a child's, and the pilot leapt to his feet. He looked out towards the reef but could see nothing, just the waves endlessly turning and falling. The pilot heard the cry again and suddenly he saw Ito thrashing madly in the water, a black dorsal fin cutting the surface.

The shark circled as it came in to attack again, the orderly crying out in terror. Strickland stood there mesmerised, unable to think or act. The fin disappeared and Ito shouted again, the scream even more terrible than before. The pilot quickly gathered his senses and dived into the water, striking out towards his friend who was desperately trying to fight off his attacker with his knife. The sea foamed red around the orderly while he repeatedly slashed at the shark, its blood mingling with his own as it continued its frenzy. Strickland swam quickly, but by the time he got to Ito the shark had disappeared, leaving him choking and sobbing in the surf. The pilot put an arm around his shoulders comforting him and started to swim back to the shore, the orderly shaking and weeping with pain as he struggled to stay afloat. Using all his strength Strickland hauled the orderly behind him, trying to shut out the agony his friend was going through. He reached the shore and gathering Ito in his arms he clambered out of the surf and made his way across the rocks, running and shouting as he went, the orderly's blood streaming down his body.

The pilot came to the end of the promontory and leaping down, he dashed across the beach, his feet sinking in the granular sand as he cradled his injured friend in his arms. Ito threw back his head and howled in agony, his body gashed and slippery with blood, his flesh hanging down in ribbons. Strickland staggered up the beach and reaching the treeline he laid the orderly down in the shade, unable to carry him any further. He told him to stay conscious and set off up the path towards the camp, crying out for Hayama.

The captain had only just returned from his butterfly

expedition and was sitting in his hut, when he heard his name being called. He could tell it was the Englishman, but why was he yelling so much? He put down his specimen box and going to the door, he saw Strickland running towards him, his body smeared in blood.

'My God! What's happened, are you hurt?' he said, descending the steps as the pilot stopped and stood there gasping for breath

'Ito ... Ito ... shark!'

'What! Where is he?'

'On the beach! ... Quickly! ...' said the pilot, his hands on his knees, his voice hoarse.

Hayama turned and shouted at some soldiers who had heard the commotion and were coming towards them.

'Bring the medical kit!' he cried and together the officers ran down towards the shore.

Ito lay there in the shade, his chest heaving as he fought against the pain which racked his body. Strickland knelt down and held his hand and Hayama spoke softly to him, telling him to be brave.

A sweating Noguchi arrived with the black medical bag and put it on the ground beside them. The captain opened it and taking out a syringe, he filled it from a morphine capsule and injected the orderly in the arm. He put the syringe aside and tied a tourniquet around Ito's left leg which was almost severed, the white knee bone exposed. He then took out a wad of dressings and placed them over the wounds in his abdomen in an attempt to staunch the flow of blood. The pilot continued to hold his friend's hand as the morphine took effect and after a while the orderly became calmer. Ito started to mutter and Strickland looked at Hayama.

'What's he saying?'

'He's praying,' the captain answered, his forearms smeared in bright arterial blood, as he pressed a dressing into the orderly's side.

The pilot gripped his friend's hand and began to pray with him, begging God to let him live. Hayama worked desperately, unwrapping more dressings and telling the pilot to help him press down on the wounds. But the orderly was losing too much blood and there was nothing the captain or anyone could do to stem the flow, as Ito gradually slipped away. Finally, his voice went quiet, his grip on Strickland's hand loosened and his body fell slack. Hayama sat back and the pilot let go of his friend's hand. Ito was dead. Silence fell among the group. No one said a word. The only sound was a faint rustle as the wind stirred the fronds of the palm trees. A sudden cry went up from the assembled soldiers, as they clasped each other and began to weep for their dead comrade.

The captain closed the medical bag and got to his feet, telling the soldiers to cover the orderly's body. They would bury him at sunset. The men did as they were told and gathered up the branches that lay scattered about and placed them over the orderly. Soon, Ito was covered with palm fronds and Hayama told two soldiers to fetch some spades and dig a grave. There would be no funeral pyre, because the smoke could be spotted from the air.

'Be sure to make it deep,' he said to the soldiers as they left.

Noguchi, his face streaked with tears, stepped foward and bowed before his captain.

'Sir, please allow me the honour of preparing the final resting place of my dear friend Private Ito.'

Hayama looked at him and nodded.

'Of course, sergeant,' he replied, before turning to the pilot who stood transfixed, staring at the body of his dead friend. 'Come on. It's not your fault. No one could have survived that.'

The captain dismissed his men and putting an arm around Strickland's shoulders, he led him back through the trees towards his cabin.

'Go and wash. I'll see you in my quarters when you're ready,' and with that Hayama trudged back to his hut and shut the door.

Strickland looked at his own body and saw that he was

covered in blood. Great red streaks ran from his chest and arms and down his shorts and legs. He went round to the shower at the back of his hut and stripping off, he washed Ito's blood from his body. He picked up his shorts and cleaned them, scrubbing the khaki material with a bar of soap. When the pilot had finished he placed them on a rail in the sun and ascended the stairs to his cabin. He pushed open the door and picking up a towel, he dried himself and then tied it around his waist. Strickland stood there forlornly, as silent and desolate as a ruin. He wondered if the orderly had known there were sharks out by the reef. Had he ignored the danger so that he could go and catch a delicacy so beloved by his captain? The pilot refused to believe it. Ito was a fisherman who knew the hazards of the sea and would not have risked his life for such a thing.

The Englishman walked over to his bed, picked up his shirt and put it on. He went to the washstand and began to comb his hair, but avoided looking into the mirror. He did not want to catch a glimpse of Ito's memory. The pilot put the comb down and sat for a while on his bed, trying to make sense of what had happened. But he could not, so he went out into the yard and finding that his shorts were almost dry, he took off his towel and put them on. He looked up and saw the sun descending westwards, the sky deepening. Above him the palms sighed in the breeze, the burnished afternoon light gilding their leaves.

A goat bleated in the yard as the pilot turned and walked towards Hayama's quarters. He ascended the steps, pushed open the fly screen and saw the captain dressed for parade, his sword hanging by his side.

'Are you ready?' he asked.

'Yes,' replied Strickland.

'Good. I shall call the men,' and going outside the captain told a soldier to get the company to fall in. The pilot followed Hayama out onto the verandah and watched as the men lined up in the square, their uniforms buttoned to the neck, their rifles by their sides.

'Present arms!' shouted the captain and the men all raised their rifles to their shoulders.

Hayama and Strickland descended the steps and at another command, the soldiers turned and wheeled. With the captain at their head and the pilot on his right, the officers led the way down to the beach. The men were silent as they marched away, there was just the steady tramp of their boots. When they reached the shore the pilot saw the grave had already been dug. Beside it lay Ito, also dressed in his green military uniform. He looked peaceful as he lay on his bier of palm leaves, as though he had died in his sleep. His arms were folded across his chest and in his hands he held an orchid. At the head of the grave someone had fashioned a rough cross from two pieces of driftwood and tied a wreath of forest flowers around it.

The men lined up opposite the grave and when they were all assembled, the captain began his eulogy. He told them how the orderly had embodied the true spirit of bushido. How he had lived to serve, always happy in his work. Hayama spoke of Ito's gifts not only as a fisherman and cook, but also as a singer and actor. He described in detail the night he had made everyone laugh as 'Sweet Pea' and how his good humour never failed him. Now he was gone. But his spirit would live on in their hearts, as he went to join his ancestors in heaven.

The company sang the national anthem *Kimigayo* and a group of men began to lower Ito into the grave with ropes. The firing party then raised their rifles and a fusillade of shots reverberated among the trees, scattering a troop of monkeys and making them scream. Strickland stood there and watched as the body of his friend disappeared into the void. When the men had finished, Hayama bowed his head and began to sing, his voice drifting across the sand towards the sea.

From Ueno Station to Kudanzaka
I get impatient, not knowing my way around.
It has taken me all day, leaning on my cane,

To come and see you, my son, at Kudanzaka.
The great gate looming up in the sky
Leads to a magnificent shrine
That enrolls my son among the gods.
Your unworthy mother weeps in her joy.
I was a black hen who gave birth to a hawk.
And such good fortune is more than I deserve.
I wanted to show you your Order of the Golden Kite,
And have come to see you, my son, at Kudanzaka.

The captain stopped singing, the sound of his voice replaced by the susurration of the waves upon the beach. Slowly, the burial party began to disperse until only Strickland and Noguchi remained. The pilot watched as the sergeant picked up a spade and began to shovel the ash-coloured earth back into the grave. Strickland took the other and together the two men silently filled the hole. When they had finished, they gathered the palm fronds and laid them on top of the mound of pale sand. His work done, the sergeant bowed and walked away, leaving Strickland alone at the graveside.

The pilot tried to pray, but no words came and so he stood silently grieving over his dead friend. He could shed no tears, instead there was just a terrible ache within. Finally, he turned away and began walking along the shore. He saw a cluster of ghost crabs feasting on something and, realising that it was a patch of Ito's blood, he kicked at them angrily and they scuttled away, their mouths bubbling, their pincers raised in defiance. Strickland climbed up the rocks of the promontory and made his way along the spur towards the wreck. He knew he would never walk this way again, but he wanted to say a last farewell to a place which they had both loved. The pilot reached the end of the promontory and looked out towards the booming surf where Ito had met his end and sitting down on the sea-wet rocks, he put his hands to face and wept.

THIRTEEN

Ito's death had a profound effect upon the camp. Whereas before the soldiers had been cheerful and performed their tasks willingly and without complaint, now there was an emptiness in their hearts and although they continued to carry out their duties, they felt no joy or sense of pride in what they did. When they were not working the soldiers hung listlessly about the compound, or else lay moribund in their bunks smoking or staring vacantly into space. There were no more games played on the beach, or horseplay off the end of the jetty. It was as if each man was simply waiting for something to happen, something that would shake them out of their torpor.

The man most affected by Ito's death was Hayama. While the captain still kept up appearances and tried to jolly his men along, inwardly he grieved. He blamed himself for the orderly's death because he knew that if Ito had not gone out to the reef to fish, he would still be alive. The orderly had once told Hayama he had seen a shark there, but said that it was only small and had probably been unable to find its way back to the open sea. The captain had told him not to take any risks and had then forgotten about it. Even so, he felt he should have reminded Ito of the danger and never to venture out as far as the reef. And because he had not, his friend was dead.

The truth was that the orderly had a special place in the camp. Not only on account of his gentle nature which endeared him to everybody, but also because he was the only soldier who had a personal relationship with Hayama. Although Ito was only a private, he was also the captain's orderly and therefore privy to his personal thoughts and occasional doubts. Hayama kept himself apart from his men on purpose, but he could not do so with his own orderly and in any case he enjoyed Ito's company. He had relied on him even more after Ensign Aoki's death, when he became the only officer in the camp. Then there was the arrival of the pilot. At first Hayama felt that his inability to execute his enemy was an unforgivable sign of weakness, but his orderly had told him that it would have been wrong to have killed the Englishman. Hayama had always wondered why, but then what cause would the pilot's death have served? Nothing. No, Ito had been right about so many things.

Strickland too felt the orderly's loss keenly and in the days after his death, he and the captain were inseparable. They shared out Ito's duties between them: Hayama cooked and washed the dishes, while the pilot tended the chickens, milked the goats and weeded the vegetable garden. He no longer went fishing by the promontory and instead he would take his rod and cast from the wooden jetty. There were fewer fish there and the ones he caught were smaller, but the other place held too many memories for him.

A week after Ito's death the pilot and the captain were sitting on the tatami finishing their breakfast with the radio playing behind them. Suddenly the music stopped and an announcer came on. Hayama was refreshing their cups of tea when he dropped the pot with a crash, the tea spilling onto the table. He leapt to his feet and going to the radio, he turned up the volume.

'What is it?' asked the pilot as the tea spread in a pool across the table.

The captain frowned and raised a finger to his lips, as he listened intently to the voice. Strickland did not understand a word of what was being said, but was aware from Hayama's expression that it was serious. Eventually the captain turned and faced him.

'They have bombed Hiroshima!'

The pilot was still unable to comprehend fully what had happened. Many Japanese cities had been bombed and were still being bombed, what was so special about Hiroshima?

'Is it bad?'

The captain shook his head and realised that the pilot had not understood the announcement.

'One bomb. The Americans have dropped a single bomb and annihilated a city.'

It was impossible, thought Strickland. Such a weapon simply did not exist.

'What do you mean? What sort of bomb?'

'They described it as a "hydrogen" bomb. It exploded with such force that it has destroyed everything.'

'Everything?'

'In the vicinity. For a radius of two or three miles. An entire city reduced to ashes.'

'Are you sure … I mean perhaps it's not true. It could be propaganda.'

The captain let out a long sigh.

'No, I am sure it's true. The announcer also repeated the Allies' demands. They have insisted upon Japan's unconditional surrender.'

The pilot got to his feet and stood there for a moment not knowing what to say.

'Hayama …'

The captain remained motionless, his face blank, his mind still numb from shock.

'I just don't understand it,' he muttered. 'Why?'

'What are you going to do?'

Hayma shrugged his shoulders and sighed.

'I shall await orders. And until I receive anything to the contrary, I shall continue with my duties here.'

'But the Allies have demanded that Japan surrender.'

The captain faced his friend, his eyes blazing with anger.

'The land of Yamato will never surrender! If the Allies want peace then they must negotiate. If they want to subjugate us they will have to invade and they will have to fight for every inch of territory!'

Strickland realised his friend was upset, but what he was suggesting was insanity.

'You cannot fight against this weapon.'

'If the same had happened to you. If Manchester or Liverpool had been destroyed, would Britain surrender without a fight?'

Hayama looked at Strickland, an honest question in his eyes to which the pilot already knew the answer.

'No,' he replied.

'Of course not! No country would.'

The captain turned and went over to the window and looked out across the compound. The camp was quiet and peaceful, and not a breath of wind stirred the green canopy of palms. The air moved in waves above the trees and the cicadas sang madly in the heat. His gaze wandered across the forest towards the mountain, which rose above the island. How he wished he was back in Japan! He hated his country suffering while he remained isolated thousands of miles away. More than ever before the captain wanted the war to be over, so that he could go back home and see his beloved parents.

'Will this madness ever end?' he sighed.

Hayama turned away from the window and faced the pilot once more.

'I must tell my men what's happened.'

'Of course.'

'Stay here. I won't be long,' and he went towards the door.

'Hayama ...'

'Yes?'

Strickland hesitated, but while the captain had been at the window, he too had been thinking. He was unsure as to how he should put it, but he knew that he had to say what was on his mind.

'I realise I owe you a debt which I cannot repay. You saved my life and have kept me here as your guest ...' The pilot paused, trying to find the right words. 'Under the Geneva Convention an officer is entitled to disobey an order, if he feels it jeopardises his life or the lives of those under his command. You do not have to wait for your government to make an announcement. Tell your men that you have decided to surrender.'

The captain stared intently at the pilot, his face expressing concern rather than contempt.

'I cannot make such a decision. Only the Emperor can do that.'

'You can surrender ...'

'And who exactly should I surrender to?'

The question remained unanswered and the two men stood facing each other, just a few feet apart. They may as well have been on opposite sides of the world, such was the chasm that lay between them. The silence was profound, like a great bell that would not toll. Eventually the Japanese officer spoke.

'Captain Tadashi Hayama does not understand such language,' and turning his back, he left his cabin and strode across the compound to the men's quarters.

The captain ascended the steps of their hut and stood at the open door. The soldiers immediately leapt from their bunks and chairs and standing before him, they all bowed in unison.

Hayama surveyed them, his hands clasped behind his back. They looked a sorry bunch, their uniforms were unbuttoned and some of them had not even bothered to shave. It had all been so different before Ito's death. Well, things were going to change.

'Honourable gentlemen,' he began. 'I have some sad news to report. The city of Hiroshima has been bombed by the Americans. They have dropped a weapon of such ferocity that virtually the entire city lies in ruins ...'

The men stood there silently, trying to take in the terrible news that Hayama had just told them. Like the pilot they wondered how a single bomb could destroy a city, but they did not doubt the veracity of the captain's words. Their officer looked at them, knowing that what he would say next would be an even greater blow.

'The Allies have also demanded that Japan surrender.'

The soldiers gasped and turned to each other. Surrender? Such a thing was impossible. They still had a navy and an air force and millions of men remained under arms. The loss of the islands in the Pacific was unfortunate, but it was not irrevocable. They would get them back. Japan had never been defeated in its history. Why should they surrender now? As the men pondered these questions, Noguchi stepped forward and bowed before his captain. Unlike the rest of the men, he was immaculately turned out as always. His uniform freshly ironed, the brass buttons of his tunic polished and gleaming.

'Captain-san, is what you say true?'

'It is.'

'Then ... we are to surrender?'

The men held their breath as the senior NCO uttered the fateful word and they all kept their eyes upon their commanding officer, waiting for his answer. Hayama looked at them and slowly shook his head.

'Only the God Emperor has the authority to demand such a thing and he has issued no such decree. Until he does the land of Yamato shall continue its glorious fight against the enemy. Long live Japan!'

'Long live Japan!' shouted the soldiers and for the first time since the orderly's death, a cheer went up and gladness returned to their faces. Once again they had something to fight for. They would fight to the end. They would never surrender!

Hayama smiled and watched them celebrate. But he still had something else to say. He waited until they had finished shouting and slapping each others' backs, and when a semblance of order returned, he began gently to admonish them, telling them it was time they returned to their old ways. He understood why they had all slackened in the past few days, but they must put the tragedy of Ito's death behind them, since they still had important work to do for the Motherland. Again the men started cheering and with the shouts still ringing in his ears, the captain left the hut and returned to his own quarters.

The officer walked across the compound and ascending the steps, he pushed opened the door of his cabin. The place was empty apart from Chamberlain who sat in a corner chittering on the end of his chain and he wondered where Strickland was. It did not matter particularly and he assumed the pilot had taken a walk or gone fishing. He had not been offended by what the Englishman said, he was sure that had the circumstances been reversed, he would have done the same. The pilot was an honourable man, he just did not understand the Japanese way of thinking. Nor was he the first Occidental to do so.

The captain took off his cap and went over to his bed. The macaque rose to its feet and he bent down and stroked its head. Then he picked up his violin and began to play, the music rising up and drifting out of the window like some exotic scent. He played until he felt his heart swell with longing, and he closed his eyes as he thought of the valleys and streams of his native land. He remembered the pines twisted and bent by the wind and the mountains capped with snow. Hayama hoped that one day soon he would be back among his own people. He made a promise that when he returned to Nagasaki, his first duty would be to pay a visit to the Suwa shrine and make an offering to the gods.

FOURTEEN

After Hayama's announcement, life in the camp returned to the rhythms and echoes it had when Ito was alive. The soldiers regained their humour and discipline and went about their tasks with their customary vigour, and the shocking news of Hiroshima and the Allies' ultimatum was, if not forgotten, then at least ignored.

That afternoon the men took their siesta as usual, playing cards and chatting and smoking cigarettes. A trio asked Noguchi if he wanted to make up a four for poker, but he declined with a smile and a shake of his head and instead remained on his bed, writing a letter to his wife. On the table beside him were two photographs, one was a formal portrait of him and his spouse taken on their wedding day and the other was of her holding a small white bundle in her arms, their son Shinzo. Noguchi had not seen him for four years. The boy was almost six now and he imagined him running and playing and doing all the things that small boys liked to do. The sergeant wondered what he would think when he met his father again. He would not recognise this strange man and perhaps he would reject him. At the very least the child would hide behind his mother's skirts.

Noguchi came from a village near Nagano in the central highlands. His father was a farmer and he would inherit his land when he died. It consisted only of a couple of paddy fields, an orchard with plums and cherries, a birch wood and a lake full of carp, but it was enough to support a small family. With his army pension he might be able to buy some more land and when his son was big enough, they could work on the farm together. He and his wife might have another boy, then he would have plenty of help. Perhaps they would have a daughter. A girl would be nice. She could help her mother in the house and darn his work clothes when they got holes. A boy and a girl would make a perfect family.

The sergeant thought about home often, especially now. It was August and the trees in the orchard would be laden with fruit. The cherries would already have been picked and the plums would be ripe, their dusky skins oozing sweet wine. Autumn was his favourite season, it was a time when all the year's hard work on the farm finally bore fruit. The grain would be drying in the barn and the grass in the orchard would be covered with windfall; wasps buzzing among the fruit as they got drunk on the fermenting juice. During the day the sun burned hotly, but in the evenings the air cooled and in the valleys a low mist formed. House martins would gather twittering on telegraph wires, the young flying to and fro, gaining strength before the October rains when they flew south for warmer climes.

Apart from his family, what the sergeant missed most in the tropics were the seasons. On the island it was always steamy and hot, the only variation in temperature was when it rained. Sometimes it poured so hard you could not see your hand in front of your face, and the wind blew with such force that it was foolish to venture out. Then the skies cleared, the sun would shine and it would seem as if the storm had never happened. The tropics had an extraordinary ability to erase their own history. Noguchi knew that when they left the island the jungle would soon encroach, green shoots would sprout from the dusty compound and the huts would become covered in creepers and eventually collapse. In a few years any trace that they had ever been there would vanish. Nature once again reclaiming what was hers.

The sergeant put down his pen and began reading his letter. Like Hayama he had received no news of his family since he had been on the island, but they had at least been able to send letters home, handing over the mail to the submarines that visited them for supplies. The last one had been I-47 and that, along with his most recent letter, was now at the bottom of ocean. Noguchi wondered when they would ever see another and with a sigh he put the letter in an envelope and wrote his address on the front. The sergeant did not seal it, but left it open for Hayama to read. It was the captain's job to censor every piece of mail. None were sent unless they had been read by him and passed with his personal stamp. Noguchi placed the letter next to the photographs of his wife and child and getting up, he put on his cap and went outside.

The heat was enervating and he longed for the cool autumn winds of home. He walked across the burning compound and took the path down to the beach, passing through the tall palms and coming to the clearing which gave way to a swath of pale sand. To one side lay Ito's grave. The flowers around the cross had withered and Noguchi decided to replace them with some fresh ones. The prettiest flowers grew further into the forest and he set off down the beach, heading into the trees above the bluff.

As the sergeant walked among the trees he gathered various flowers for his garland: a sprig of frangipani here, an orchid there, a stem of heliconia. When he had picked enough flowers, he sat down on a rock and began to twist them together in a bright wreath. A wreath fit for any hero, a wreath for his friend Ito. With the garland finished Noguchi got up and made his way along the path to the shrine. Shadows fell across the narrow trail as he walked, and forest birds whistled and cried, shaking their brilliant plumage as they flitted among the trees. When he reached the shrine he removed his cap and placed an orchid in the Buddha's lap. The golden god smiled serenely at him and taking a step back, the sergeant bowed his head and began to pray, holding the wreath before him. He wondered what sort of heaven his friend inhabited. Was it a Christian heaven or was it nirvana? He did not know. But he was sure that whatever afterlife there was, Ito was there in peace with his ancestors.

Noguchi finished praying and came away from the shrine with a sense of relief, as if a burden had been lifted or a problem resolved. It was curious, but he felt like this only after he prayed. The only other time he had experienced a similar feeling was after his first taste of action in Manchuria. They had fought the Chinese for three days and nights in the depths of winter. His regiment had endured an artillery barrage of unbelievable ferocity and had beaten off wave after wave of attacks. Then early one morning as they waited for the next assault at dawn, they looked over the parapet of their trenches to find that the Chinese had withdrawn, leaving the battlefield strewn with hundreds of corpses. The only sound was the wind polishing the empty sky and the harsh cry of crows, feasting on the bloated bodies of the Kuomintang.

The sergeant walked back along the beach, the surf lapping the shore in a constant and unrequited caress. He reached Ito's grave and removing the withered remains of the old wreath, he replaced it with the new one. He then stood back and bowed before the cross. Noguchi remained like this for some time, before finally straightening and with a last salute, he marched away towards the camp. Behind him stood the cross, marking the grave of his dead friend. Around it hung the wreath, its flowers trembling in the sea breeze.

FIFTEEN

In the early morning mineral light, Strickland stood at the end of the pier and cast his lure into the clear waters of the harbour. The catch at his feet gleamed, the fish occasionally twitching, their gills flexing as they expired in the cool air. They were mostly young mullet which he had enticed towards the jetty, by throwing balls of rice into the water. Each time he threw a morsel into the harbour, the surface would swirl briefly as the fish devoured the pale offering. The lesser ones attracted the larger fish and it was these the pilot hoped to catch, although so far he had only hooked small fry. He glanced down at the haul of silver at his feet and decided that he had enough for Hayama and himself.

The pilot reeled in his lure and picking up his catch, he put the rod over his shoulder and walked back along the jetty, the fish flashing like coins in the sun. He strode across the beach and taking the path that led to the camp, he made his way to the yard behind the huts. When he got there Strickland leant his rod against the wall of his cabin and laid his catch on a table. He pulled a knife from his pocket and began to gut and fillet the fish, throwing the entrails to the chickens which clucked and fought over them in the dust. When he had finished he took the fillets and hung them on a long bamboo pole to dry in the sun, just as Ito had done.

Strickland plunged his hands into a bucket of rainwater and washed the fish scale and slime from his fingers. He shook them dry and ascended the steps of his quarters, keen to get out of the sun which now rose rapidly into the morning sky. Inside, the hut was pleasantly cool and going over to the pitcher on the table, the pilot poured himself a glass of water. He went to his desk, sat down and opened a large Japanese-English dictionary that belonged to Hayama. He had set himself the task of learning a hundred words of vocabulary a day, which he would then use in conversation with his friend, the captain correcting his pronunciation and grammar.

Sometimes they would go for long walks together. As they walked the pilot would point to various trees, birds and flowers and ask Hayama for the words in Japanese. Once they made their way up to the top of the mountain, which Strickland had not visited since his first day of freedom. They stood together on the observation platform admiring the view, the sea stretching before them like a sheet of beaten tin. In the distance a ship drew a pale arabesque in the blue ocean as it steamed north. The captain pointed out the other islands and atolls, naming the larger ones. His companion asked him if there were any other observation posts out there and Hayama smiled enigmatically.

Strickland spent the morning in his cabin, writing down various words and phrases from the dictionary which he intended to use with his friend. He would diligently set himself a different task each day; sometimes he would construct small phrases of enquiry, other times he would choose a subject and methodically translate the necessary vocabulary. Japanese, like Chinese as Strickland discovered, often had many different pronunciations of a single word or character, so that the slightest nuance could change its meaning completely. His occasional difficulties had given Hayama cause for considerable hilarity. As the captain rocked back and forth with mirth the pilot would sit there bemused, aware that he had made yet another solecism.

At midday Strickland heard footsteps outside his quarters. He looked up and saw Hayama standing at the door.

'Hello there,' he said, as his friend approached.

The captain did not reply and simply held out his arms.

'Are you all right?' asked the pilot, concerned at his friend's silence. He got to his feet and walked towards him and could see the captain's face was wet with tears. 'What is it, Hayama? What's the matter?'

'Nagasaki …' he gasped, his voice choked with grief. 'They have bombed Nagasaki!'

SIXTEEN

It is the end. Everyone on the island knows this. No one can tell precisely at what hour the final moment will come, but they are resigned to it just as the condemned are resigned to their fate. There is no power on earth now which can change the outcome. The gods themselves have decided. Whatever shall be, shall be. Just as the carp fights furiously after it is caught by the fisherman, when it is placed upon the slab it patiently awaits death, knowing that it is useless to struggle.

Hayama is sitting at his desk. Ever since the bombing of Nagasaki, he has had the radio on at all hours. He has barely slept all week. He is listening for the inevitable announcement. Like the carp on the slab he too has stopped struggling and accepts his fate. There is a serenity about the captain as he sits there with the monkey on his lap, stroking its soft fur, the macaque oblivious to his master's predicament and the enormity of what is about to happen. The captain is waiting for an announcement by the Emperor, which will come at any moment. He listens to the national radio station NHK and at midday the presenter comes on the air:

'*This will be a broadcast of the gravest importance. Will all listeners please rise. His Majesty the Emperor will now read his imperial transcript to the people of Japan. We respectfully transmit his voice ...*'

Kimigayo is played and when it has finished the emperor's recorded message begins. His voice, which has never been broadcast before, is high-pitched and fluting. It is the Voice of the Crane.

'*To My Good and Loyal Subjects: After pondering deeply the general trends of the world and the actual conditions obtaining in Our Empire today, I have decided to effect of the present an extraordinary measure ...'*

Hayama stands there, his head bowed, his hands by his side as he listens in reverent silence. The Emperor continues to speak, giving his subjects the order which all expected would come, but who are still shocked when it is finally announced.

'The striving for peace and well-being of our imperial subjects, and the sharing of common happiness and prosperity amongst tens of thousands of nations is the duty left by our Imperial Ancestors, and I am the one who has not forgotten about this duty ...

In addition the enemy has recently used a most cruel explosive. The frequent killing of innocents and the effect of destitution it entails are incalculable. Should we continue fighting in the war, it would not only cause the complete annihilation of our nation, but also the destruction of human civilisation. With this in mind, how should I save billions of our subjects and their posterity, and atone ourselves before the hallowed spirits of Our Imperial Ancestors? This is the reason why I ordered the Imperial Government to accept the Joint Declaration ...

We have resolved to pave the way for a grand peace for all generations to come by enduring the unendurable and suffering what is insufferable, for peace to last thousands of generations ...'

The captain has his orders, it is his duty now to carry them out. When the broadcast finishes Hayama straightens and replaces his cap. He goes to the door, calls out to one of the guards and tells him to get the men to fall in. The man runs off to the soldiers' quarters and they quickly file out and assemble in front of their captain. Hayama stands there on the verandah and when they are all arrayed, he descends the steps and addresses them.

'Honourable gentlemen, it has been a great privilege to be your commanding officer and to have worked with you over these past years. We have performed an invaluable service to the

Motherland of which we can justly be proud. Now our work is done and it is time for all of us to go home …'

The captain continues speaking, the men listening silently. Above them the imperial flag of the rising sun hangs limply on its pole. He tells them of the Emperor's announcement that Japan has agreed to the terms of the Allies' Joint Declaration and that the war is now over. They are to leave the island immediately and should take nothing with them. Hayama thanks his men once more and some of them begin to weep. After a command from Noguchi, they all bow at their commander and he returns their salute.

'Let us sing our glorious national anthem together one last time,' their officer says and the company begins to sing *Kimigayo*, their voices resonant and tuneful.

> *The Emperor's reign will last*
> *For a thousand and then eight thousand generations*
> *Until pebbles become mighty rocks*
> *Covered with moss.*

When they finish the men give three cheers and salute their captain one last time, and with Noguchi at their head, they proceed to march away. Hayama watches them go, his heart full of pride. How is it possible that he has been able to command such men? Truly he has been blessed. As they disappear down the path towards the beach, the captain turns and goes back inside his hut. He still has one final task.

It is hot and Hayama wants to be properly prepared. He takes off his uniform and puts on his kimono, tying the cord around his waist. He picks up a pair of scissors and after cutting off a lock of hair, he proceeds to clip his fingernails. When he has finished he carefully puts the clippings and the hair in a jar on his desk. He then sits down and picks up a pen. He thinks for a few moments, before writing a last haiku.

As a peony dissolves
In the flames
So too my beloved city
Is reduced to ashes.

The captain looks at what he has written and satisfied, he gets up and goes over to the rack of swords by his bed. Above them is his icon of St John. He stands there and bows low before the saint. He straightens and picks up both the *katana* and the *tanto* and goes and sits down on the tatami. He lays the swords next to him, then draws the *tanto* from its scabbard. Hayama undoes the cord of his kimono, exposing his bare midriff. He takes up the dagger and plunges it into his belly and with both hands upon the hilt, he draws it firmly across his gut in a single stroke. He does not cry out, but gives a sharp intake of breath, like the final gasp of a drowning man.

Strickland is fishing off the edge of the pier when he hears the soldiers' boots tramping across the wooden jetty. He turns and sees them assemble by the patrol boat as, one by one, they begin to board. He reels in his line, puts the rod over his shoulder and walks towards them, curious to know what is going on. The pilot approaches Noguchi with a bemused look on his face.

'What's all this, sergeant?'

The NCO bows at the Englishman, before answering him.

'The war is over, Mr Strickland ...'

'When did this happen?'

'Just now. Captain Hayama-san told us.'

The pilot looks at the men boarding the patrol boat and is still confused.

'What are they doing?'

'The captain says we must leave. Our work here finished. We return home.'

'But what about the captain? Is he not coming too?'

The sergeant looks at the Englishman, who obviously does not understand.

'Captain Hayama-san …' he begins, before pausing to search for words in a language that is not his own. 'Captain Hayama-san … has other duties.'

Strickland does not reply, but drops the rod and begins running down the jetty. Noguchi watches him go, knowing that he is too late. The sergeant turns and walking up the gangplank, he pulls it in behind him and tells his men to cast off. The ropes are dropped and the patrol boat's motor roars into life as the vessel eases away from the pier. The grey boat chugs across the still, clear waters of the harbour, before making its way through the surrounding reef and heading out into the open sea.

The pilot sprints across the sand and races up through the trees towards the compound and Hayama's hut. As he approaches the air is filled with shrill, demented screams. It sounds as though a child is being murdered and, running up the steps of the captain's quarters, Strickland is confronted by the sight of Chamberlain shrieking wildly and tugging at his chain. Beside him is Hayama, dressed in his kimono and sitting cross-legged on the tatami, his head hanging on his chest. Hearing the pilot enter, he looks up and smiles.

'I knew you'd come.'

'What on earth's going on?'

'I'm sorry about the terrible noise. I forgot to release Chamberlain. Can you let him go?'

Strickland stoops and unties the macaque's collar and the monkey springs up onto the windowsill and baring his teeth in a grimace, he takes one final look at the scene and flees. The pilot sees that the captain's kimono is soaked crimson, the bloody dagger on the floor beside him.

'My God! What have you done?' he says, kneeling before his friend.

'I have just one request,' the captain whispers, indicating the *katana* in front of him. 'If you would grant me the honour.'

The pilot looks at the sword and recoils in horror, as though he has been asked to pick up a snake.

'No, Hayama, I can't. I cannot do it.'

'Please … you must,' and his friend looks beseechingly at him.

Strickland knows that he is in agony, his brow is twisted with pain. Yet he cannot bring himself to pick up the sword.

'No … no, I can't.'

The captain realises the Englishman is struggling against his better nature, but he wants him to understand he is doing the right thing. That it is his destiny. Hayama looks at the man who has been so many things to him and he remembers something else. The words of the little friar.

'In the evening of life we shall be examined in love.'

Strickland gazes into his friend's eyes, eyes that are filled with pain and the realisation of what he has to do dawns upon him. It is the final act of friendship. Hayama nods and smiles, and leaning forward, he begins to pray. The pilot picks up the *katana* and gets to his feet. The sword is weightless in his hands. It has become part of him. He raises the blade above his head and brings it down upon the captain's neck, decapitating him with a single blow.

The Englishman cannot recall what happened next, it is as if he has been inhabiting a dream. He finds himself alone upon the beach, walking barefoot across the burning sand. In his hand he holds a sword. The surf booms in the distance. He looks out across the water and sees the blue band of the horizon quivering like a violin to the sea's music.

ACKNOWLEDGEMENTS

I would like to thank Group Captain Rob Caddick and Squadron Leader Al Pinner who made useful comments and corrections to the typescript of the first edition, concerning the RAF and its wartime history. In particular I am indebted to Squadron Leader Pinner, Commanding Officer of the Battle of Britain Memorial Flight, for sharing his knowledge of Spitfires and their technical performance. I would also like to thank the staff at the Imperial War Museum and the National Army Museum in London for their help. Finally, this book would not have been written without the memory of my grandfather Lt Col Tom Guise Tucker MC, a Burma veteran who brought home a samurai sword and told me its story.